SUDDENLY FRANÇOISE PULLED ON MY sleeve. "Linc! Look outside."

I glanced up, but the light inside the restaurant made it so I was looking at my own reflection in the window.

My reflection moved, but I didn't.

Then it gave me a stern stare down. Benjamin Green-style. He was right outside!

F. T. BRADLEY

HARPER

An Imprint of HarperCollins*Publishers*

Library of Congress Cataloging-in-Publication Data

Bradley, F. T.

    Double vision / F. T. Bradley. — 1st ed.

        p.   cm.

    Summary: "After a routine school field trip goes awry, Linc Baker is thrust into a world of intrigue and espionage, where a kid agent who looks exactly like him threatens to use powerful artifacts to control the world"— Provided by publisher.

  ISBN 978-0-06-210438-0

  [1. Adventure and adventurers—Fiction. 2. Impersonation—Fiction. 3. Spies—Fiction. 4. Paris (France)—Fiction. 5. France—Fiction.] I. Title.

PZ7.B7246Do   2012   2012005734

[Fic]—dc23   CIP

                                                    AC

Typography by Lissi Erwin

13 14 15 16 17   OPM   10 9 8 7 6 5 4 3 2 1

❖

First paperback edition, 2013

To Jason

PROLOGUE

IT ALL STARTED WITH A FIELD TRIP. AND BEFORE
you start expecting stuff about Greek gods or me being bitten
by a spider that turned me into some kind of superhero—
sorry to disappoint you. This isn't one of those stories. At
least my field trip wasn't to a museum, but it wasn't anywhere
cool like Universal Studios either. I go to Lompoc Middle
School in California, where expectations are high, but the
budget is low. So for our field trip, we went to a chicken farm.
Which actually turned out to change my life.

   I wouldn't even start with my field trip to the Johnson
chicken farm, but it's how it all began. How I got to be in
deep trouble, the kind that gets you grounded for a lifetime,
and how I had to go to the other side of the world to fix it.
How I got to be Benjamin Green for a week. You won't know
who he is yet, but I'll tell you all about him soon.

**PLACE: THE JOHNSON CHICKEN FARM IN
LOMPOC, CALIFORNIA, MY HOMETOWN.**

TIME: FRIDAY BEFORE THANKSGIVING BREAK.

Here's how it all went down.

1

FRIDAY, 8 A.M.

THE BUS DROPPED US AT THE CHICKEN farm at o'dark thirty, or at least it felt that way. I'm not sure who came up with seven in the morning starts for middle schoolers, but they should be forced to get up at six for a while when it's foggy and dark out. And smell chicken poop by eight.

"Now remember, kids," Mrs. Valdez said as the bus driver pulled onto the gravel driveway, "no horseplay. Listen to Mr. Johnson. Make notes in your fieldwork journal." She wagged her finger in the air.

Daryl jumped up next to me. "Yes, ma'am." He saluted Mrs. Valdez. Daryl is the kind of guy who always acts like he's had one bowl of Lucky Charms too many for breakfast.

He's also one of my best friends.

"All right, let's go," Mrs. Valdez announced. She gave me a frown. "And Lincoln."

That's me. "Yeah—I mean, yes, Mrs. Valdez?"

"Can I count on you to behave?" She gave me one of those death-ray looks. Mrs. Valdez had reason to be worried. On the last field trip when a kid from another school called Daryl a name I won't repeat, I started a tomato food fight. It was loads of fun, but my parents had to pay for the lost fruit (apparently tomatoes are a fruit, not a veggie) and cleanup. At the grocery store field trip, I set off the Code Adam alert when we couldn't find my other friend Sam, so customers were trapped for an hour (the Code Adam alert thing works great, in case you're wondering). As it turned out, Sam was just taking a bathroom break, so he wasn't actually kidnapped. But he could've been! So anyway, I'm Mrs. Valdez's field trip nightmare.

"I'll be good," I said, and I really wanted to be.

The class gathered on a small field in front of a white house with a saggy front porch, with a whole bunch of huge barns to our right, a silo to the left. And a pungent stink, with the faint noise of chickens in the background. The promise of another great sixth-grade field trip.

"All right, kids," Mrs. Valdez called. "This is Mr. Johnson." She pointed to this huge guy in overalls next to her, with thinning brown bed-head hair. He just nodded. "He's going to show us around his farm."

2

"Bawk!" That was Daryl. He was really nailing the whole chicken impersonation, let me tell you.

Mrs. Valdez didn't think it was so great, because she tossed Daryl a death-ray look. "And you'll all be silent, because we don't want to scare the chickens."

"Shut up, or they don't lay eggs," Mr. Johnson said, obviously not happy that we were there. "And no one goes near the chickens."

This confused even Mrs. Valdez. "But aren't the chickens part of the farm?"

Farmer Johnson shook his head. "The agreement was a tour of the business. No going near the barns!"

It was pretty obvious that the guy wasn't going to change his mind. So we moved along, listening to the farmer drone on about feces (this would be poop) of the not-to-be-seen chickens, the egg storage temperature, blah, blah. If this tour got any more boring, I think we all would've turned into zombies—in fact, most of the class looked sort of undead when, at eleven thirty, we took a break for lunch on the wet grass.

"Man, I think I aged a year listening to that guy," Sam complained. "Did you hear how he barked at Mrs. Valdez?"

"The guy should just marry his chickens," Daryl joked as he stole the apple from my lunch box.

I was itching to move. "Let's check out these famous chickens," I said, pointing to the giant red barns.

"Is this going to be one of your Linc disasters?" Sam asked.

"After the whole tomato mess, Mom told me to stay away."

"*Linc disasters*? That's what she called them?" I was actually hurt.

"I'm out, too, man," Daryl said, chewing my apple. "I don't need any more detention."

"Don't you want to see the chickens?"

Both Daryl and Sam shook their heads.

"Fine." I took off on my own, feeling their eyes on my back. It was almost a dare now—you get that, right? I had to go see those chickens.

I made my way over to the first barn and looked in through the narrow window. The place was stacked with cages full of chickens. They were crammed in so tight, you could barely tell where one hen ended and the other began. A conveyer belt ran underneath and behind, where eggs rolled down, away from the cages, and into a dark space I couldn't see from where I stood.

This was just wrong. No wonder Farmer Johnson didn't want us to get near the chickens. Look how he was mistreating them!

I heard a woman's voice come from behind the house. Mrs. Valdez appeared, deep in conversation with Farmer Johnson. Trying to stay out of sight, I moved around to the far side of the chicken barn, where these giant double doors were open just about an inch or so.

"If they could see the chickens, it would really make this excursion worth it," Mrs. Valdez said. She sounded way too close for comfort.

I pried the barn doors open with my fingers, and sneaked in. The poop smell was plain overwhelming, so I tried holding my breath, but that only worked for so long. A person does have to breathe. One of the chickens made a noise and pooped. Then another did the same: chirp, then poop. Chirp, poop.

I backed away, only to feel something jam into my spine. It was some giant lever.

"No," I heard Farmer Johnson say. "Nobody gets near my chickens."

One of the chickens looked at me, all ticked off, like it was my idea to put it in a cage. I looked at the big lever I'd backed into. You didn't need to be an expert on egg farming to know that it opened all the cages.

"Well, I suppose we'll be on our way, then, Mr. Johnson," Mrs. Valdez said in a sour voice.

The class was leaving. I watched Mrs. Valdez pass by the little window and walk to the field. She clapped her hands, then said something I couldn't make out.

I had to get back!

I started toward the barn doors, but then I saw that lever again. If only I had walked away and joined my class, the rest of this adventure never would've happened.

But that lever was just asking to be pushed, right?

I went over there and pushed it, sending a cloud of white feathers swirling around the barn like a tornado. *"Baaaawwwkkkk!"* The cackling was so loud, I swore it nearly broke my eardrums before I hurried out through the barn doors.

But then, so did the chickens. Dozens and dozens of bawking, squawking chickens, clawing their way to freedom. I got away from the hens and ran to the field, where Mrs. Valdez was lining up the kids. She looked horrified and waved her arms.

Farmer Johnson walked out of the house only to be hit by the chickens full force. They were digging their nails into his arms, legs, and back. Farmer Johnson started screaming like a little kid.

I laughed. Let's be honest, the guy deserved it for cramming them in cages like that. But then a few of the chickens started attacking me.

I ran in circles, trying to get away from those mad hens. "Shoo!" I yelled. "Get back!" But the chickens were looking at me like I was a great big bowl of chicken feed. The entire class was now staring at me.

"Help, it's a chicken attack!" I yelled.

But instead of helping me, the kids backed away. Sam started laughing.

"This is not funny!" I yelled. More chickens surrounded me and pecked my toes. *"Oweeee!"* I hollered, bouncing on my feet, making the class crack up even more. Then one chicken managed to land on my shoulder. And another on my head. White feathers flew all around me.

The chicken on my head turned, digging its nails into my scalp. It chirped, and I knew what came after that. You remember, right? Chirp, poop.

I howled. And the chicken pooped, all down my face.

Down my eyelashes and on my nose.

The class broke out laughing and screaming. "Hey," Daryl called from the back of the line. "It's Linc the Chicken Boy! Bawk, bawk!"

2

FRIDAY, 12:30 P.M.

I WILL SPARE YOU THE DETAILS OF HOW long it took to get the chickens to stop pecking at my head (very long) and how hard it was to rinse the chicken poop from my hair (very hard). Mrs. Valdez and I helped Mr. Johnson get the chickens back in the barn, but it was just a giant, white feathery and poopy mess in the end.

We left at twelve thirty, while Mr. Johnson was still looking for half a dozen missing hens. I secretly hoped they flew far, far away and were free to lay eggs wherever they pleased.

Mrs. Valdez made me sit in front with her for the ride back to school. The bus driver wrinkled his nose when he smelled me, but he didn't say anything.

"Well," Mrs. Valdez said after giving me the silent treatment most of the way, "I'm sure that will go down in history as the worst field trip ever."

I shrank down in my seat. "Worse than the tomato food fight?"

"Yes."

"Worse than the Code Adam alert?"

Mrs. Valdez made a groaning noise that sounded like she was falling apart.

"Are you okay, Mrs. Valdez?" I felt bad now. Mrs. Valdez had stuck her neck out for me many times, bargaining for me with the principal, giving me second, third, fourth chances. She sighed and was silent for what seemed like forever. "You know, Lincoln, if anyone asked me who my favorite student is, I would say it was you."

I laughed, but then realized she wasn't kidding. "But my grades are awful." I looked over at Mrs. Valdez. There was a tiny white feather stuck in her graying hair. "I'm your worst student."

"It's not just about grades, though, Lincoln. Sure, there are those kids who get the As, and that's wonderful. But none are as sharp as you. You see your knowledge in the context of the world."

"I don't even know what that means." The bus stopped in front of the school.

Mrs. Valdez gave me a sad and tired smile. "It doesn't matter." She sighed. Again. "I can't help you anymore—do you understand that? It's too big this time, the trouble you've caused."

Mrs. Valdez got off the bus, leaving me there, smelling like chicken poop. Sam high-fived me as he passed.

"Chicken Boyyy!" Daryl called as he rushed past, careful not to touch me. "That was awesome."

For some reason, I didn't feel so good about my Linc disaster. I waved and laughed along with my friends, but I had a feeling in my gut that maybe I'd overdone it this time.

My feeling was right.

Dad was waiting when I finally got off the bus. He wore his baggy brown carpenter pants that looked like they belonged to someone else and a white T-shirt with Baker Autos on it. Dad jingled his keys, the ones on the giant key chain with the small metal compass clipped on it, the compass Grandpa gave him when he was in Boy Scouts. He pushed his black plastic-framed glasses up the bridge of his nose. I couldn't tell if he was mad, but figured he had to be.

"Hi, Dad."

"Hi, Lincoln." He studied my head. "Did those chickens break your skin?"

"Yeah." I rubbed my scalp, where I could feel tiny scabs.

"You're lucky you've already had your tetanus shot." He opened the passenger-side door. "We better get you home and get some alcohol on that. Mom's orders."

"You told her about today?"

Dad smiled, but it wasn't a happy kind of smile. "The school called her. At work."

I groaned as we both got in the car. I tossed my backpack and skateboard on the backseat. "What'd she say?"

Dad started the car but waited before putting it in drive. "I would yell at you right now, but I know that your mom will do enough of that for both of us." He drove away from the school. "Just answer me one thing: Why did you think it was a good idea to let a barn full of chickens out?"

Honestly, after all the commotion of the day, I had no idea what had possessed me. I shrugged. "I don't know."

Dad nodded. I don't know if he got it, but he didn't ask any more questions the rest of the way home. We just listened to some old geezer rock and let the wind blow through the car so neither one of us had to smell me.

Mom is a nurse, which means she works weird hours and always walks like she's in a hurry. Plus she's working on her degree to be a nurse-practitioner, so between work and school, she pretty much runs all the time. Mom had just come off her shift when we got home around one, and she was waiting in my room, ready to let me have it.

I'll save you the whole Linc-Is-in-Trouble-Again speech, because if you've ever been in trouble, you know what those sound like.

Here's the recap.

1. I was grounded for the rest of the year (it was November, but still).

2. No TV, even though all these new shows are on (an argument that fell on deaf ears with Mom).

3. No skateboarding (my sole mode of transportation). Not that it mattered—see number one.

4. No going over to Daryl's, who has an Xbox, unlike me. So no video games, even if I just got to level five on Racing Mania Seven (another argument that fell on deaf ears).

"So what am I supposed to do for the rest of the year?" I sounded a little whiny, I'll admit, but then what *was* I supposed to do?

"Read those books Grandpa bought you for your birthday." Mom pointed to my bookshelf to *The History of Crime*, volumes one, two, and three. I could hardly wait. "Oh, and you'll help me when I have to take Grandpa to his appointments." This was the opposite of fun.

I moaned. Bad move.

"You have yourself to thank for this. You're suspended from school, Linc. Indefinitely." Mom tucked her hair behind her ears. She looked stressed out, but then that was probably my fault. "We have a meeting with the principal on Monday. I can only hope they'll take you back. I wouldn't."

"Thanks, Mom."

"You're welcome." She got up and touched my face. "I love you, Lincoln. But you sure are a handful. And take a shower—you smell."

So I did. Once I was no longer smelly, I cleaned my room (pure guilt and sucking up to Mom), only taking a break at six because it was time for dinner. All that afternoon, the phone was ringing, but I didn't think anything of it. Not until

I clearly heard some guy leave a message on the machine about an appointment regarding an "urgent legal matter."

"What's with that?" I asked Mom as she was stirring the spaghetti sauce for dinner.

"The appointment is tonight, with a lawyer. We're getting sued." She looked at me, and for the first time since I could remember, she looked scared. "That farmer wants us to pay for the chicken farm damages."

I felt like someone had punched me in the chest. "He can't do that. Right?"

Mom didn't answer me but turned her attention to dinner.

"He can't do that," I repeated, but of course he could. This is America. "What's going to happen?"

"I've never been sued before, Linc, so I don't know." Mom put the spoon down. "I guess we'll find out soon enough."

The doorbell rang, making me jump. "I'll get it," I said, trying to be helpful and suck up.

I made my way to the door. When I opened it, I heard the noise and laughter before I saw them. Chickens—or at least two kids in homemade chicken suits, with feathers taped to paper plates or something. A boom box played the chicken dance song.

"Hey, Chicken Boy!" I recognized Daryl's voice. "Wanna dance?" The other chicken suit broke out laughing. That was Sam.

All right, so that was pretty funny, right? I could've come up with that prank myself if it had been Daryl or Sam getting into chicken farm trouble. But for some reason, monkeying around with my friends was the last thing I wanted to do. "Funny, guys." I slammed the door, but I could still hear them laughing and cackling.

"Who's that at the door?" Grandpa asked. He glanced over my shoulder, out the little window next to the front door. Grandpa is old, but he can sneak up on you like a ninja. Very creepy.

"It's just my friends."

"Huh." Grandpa shrugged, then shuffled away.

The chicken dance music stopped. When I was sure they were gone, I walked to the kitchen, hoping to find some snacks to fill the pit inside my stomach.

"Dinner's on the table in twenty minutes," Mom said behind me when she saw me rummaging inside the fridge. "No snacking."

"Wasn't there a cheese ball in here the other day?" I picked up a carton of eggs to see the back of the fridge.

"No snacking!" She closed the fridge, leaving me in the snack-free kitchen, holding a carton of eggs. The doorbell rang. Again.

"Oh no, you don't," I mumbled, laughing. I walked to the door, opening up the egg carton. I took out four of them, two in each hand. I placed the carton near the door for extra ammo and opened the door.

And threw the eggs. "Crack this, you suckers!" I laughed.

It wasn't until I turned on the porch light that I realized it wasn't my friends who had rung the doorbell. There was a guy, bald, in a black suit, and a tall woman, also in a black suit, with brown hair in a bun.

"Is this the Baker residence?" Egg yolk was dripping down the bald man's face.

"Um. Yeah?"

"We're government agents." He flashed a badge. "Are you Lincoln Baker?"

3

I'D JUST EGGED THE GOVERNMENT, SO I
apologized.

"Let's cut the nonsense. Is there somewhere we can talk?"
Guy Agent asked. "Privately?"

"Um, I dunno." I should explain my domestic situation.
My house is basically a rectangle, three bedrooms, one
bathroom, an eat-in kitchen, and small living room, where
Dad was watching TV just then. So when the government
agent asked if there was somewhere private we could talk, I
almost laughed. "How about right here?"

Lady Agent settled at the end of the porch, looking
miffed.

"Lincoln Baker," Guy Agent said, like he was still not sure.

"In the flesh."

"I'm Agent Fullerton." He shook my hand, quick but firm enough to hurt. "This is Agent Stark," he said, waving behind him. Agent Stark just stared at me. "We're with a top secret special ops team called Pandora."

"You're spies?"

"We prefer 'secret agents.'"

Could this be a joke? If so, it was a good one. "So what's so top secret that brings you here? Did someone lose Pandora's box?"

Agent Fullerton kept studying my face with a smile. "It's uncanny. Isn't it, Stark?" He looked over his shoulder.

Agent Stark stood, holding a small yellow pad, looking cranky. "Uncanny," Agent Fullerton mumbled, still staring at me. He whipped out a tape measure. "Can you stand up a little straighter?" I stretched out my arms, like that would help. "Shy two inches."

Stark motioned to the white plastic lawn chairs on the porch. "You can sit now."

I felt a jolt of irritability run up my spine. "I'm okay standing, thanks. So what does the government want with me? Did one of those chickens make it across the state line or something?"

Agent Fullerton gave me a laugh, high and fake. "Funny. No, Lincoln." He dug into his breast pocket and pulled out a photograph. Handed it to me.

"What's this?" I looked at the grainy picture of a kid, in black cargo pants and a black polo shirt. He had dark hair, blue eyes—and he looked just like me, just a lot more serious. "There's this blond streak down the front of his hair, but . . ."

"Looks just like you, right?" Agent Fullerton looked excited. "Uncanny."

"What? Everyone has a double." I handed the creepy picture back and sat down in one of the plastic lawn chairs. "Why are you here?"

"One of the kids from your class stuck a video of you at the chicken farm on YouTube. Our scanning software has been searching for a match, but we didn't think you'd be this close." Agent Fullerton tucked the picture back in his pocket. "We're here to make you an offer. The kid in the picture is Benjamin Green. He's one of Pandora's top secret agents— and he's gone . . . missing."

"That's a real bummer," I said, hoping to sound tough. "But what does that have to do with me?"

Agent Fullerton glanced at Agent Stark, and she gave him a nod. "Ben is part of an undercover operation we've been running, very hush-hush. We were ready to take down a dangerous criminal organization when he went missing."

"Missing how?"

Agent Fullerton hesitated. "He last reported to me near the Louvre Museum almost two days ago. We don't know what happened to him."

"The point is," Agent Stark said, sounding impatient,

"Benjamin Green was supposed to deliver . . . a package. And then the receiving party would give him something in return."

"So it's a trade." These two agents made everything sound complicated.

"Right."

"What's in the package?" I asked.

"That information is distributed on a need-to-know basis." Agent Fullerton coughed. "You see the bind we're in, right? Without Benjamin Green in place, the exchange is off, and we have to start all over. Hundreds of man-hours—poof." He raised his hand, like an explosion. "Wasted."

"So you want me to pretend to be this junior government agent Ben kid. Like a double agent—no, an agent double." It was confusing.

"Benjamin Green, yes. Just until the exchange is done."

"And he's missing, probably taken by some guy he crossed on this case you're talking about. Right?" I watched lots of crime shows with my grandpa, so I thought I knew a thing or two about bad guys.

"Forget it, Fullerton," Agent Stark said, startling us both. She tucked her small yellow pad inside her coat pocket. "The kid doesn't want to do it. And he couldn't do the job anyway. This is a bad idea."

"It is." Even I knew that.

"But you'll be great—you have to do this!" Agent Fullerton said, looking desperate to convince his partner and me. "Plus, I never told you what you would get in return."

"What?"

"Never mind the deal." Agent Stark shook her head. "You don't want to do this, so why should we divulge any more highly classified information?"

"Wait, what's the deal?" I stood up from my chair, making it fall down on the porch floor with a thud, stopping both government agents in their tracks.

Agent Fullerton looked at his partner, then stepped closer. "You do this, we'll take care of your chicken farm business. Our intel is that this Farmer Johnson has hired Zachary Quinn."

"What?" I felt sick. So that was the lawyer Mom was meeting tonight. Zachary Quinn is one of those slick guys you always see on TV, ready to sue the pants off anyone he thinks he can get money from. I thought about how we Bakers wouldn't survive a lawsuit, since we could barely afford the groceries, let alone a lawyer. How we might even lose the house because that's all we owned.

"Your family is in for some fun." Agent Fullerton looked annoyingly smug. "These types of lawyers specialize in making your life miserable, ensuring you're broke and homeless by the time they're through with you."

Agent Stark nodded.

I thought of my parents and how they'd already dealt with so much misery over my antics. "You would make this lawsuit go away?" I asked. "If I agree to take this junior agent Benjamin Green's place?"

Agent Fullerton shrugged. "Of course." Like it was the

most normal thing in the world.

"And then I get to come back home after."

"That's right," Agent Stark said. "You come with us, be Ben for a week, and we'll make it so that chicken farm business never happened." She stepped closer. "But you do the job first. When you're done, we take care of that farmer and his ambulance-chasing lawyer. No sooner."

Now, this is what you would call an impossible dilemma. Right? I agree to this, and my family's troubles will be taken care of, but I would put my life in danger. I don't do this, the Bakers might be bankrupt and homeless.

What would you do?

Here's what I did: I stalled by asking questions. "Where am I going exactly?"

Agent Fullerton shook his head. "Can't tell you that. Not until your parents sign some paperwork."

"Can I think about it?" I asked.

"We need an answer now. Time is of the essence here." So much for stalling. Agent Fullerton stepped closer. "Are you in or out?"

I hesitated.

"Linc!" Mom called from inside the house. "Dinner!"

Thinking of Mom, Dad, and Grandpa, waiting for me over the standard Friday spaghetti dinner, I knew there really was only one choice. "I'm in."

4

PLACE: MY BEDROOM

TIME: SATURDAY, 10:30 A.M.

STATUS: NAPPING ON PAGE THREE OF *THE HISTORY OF CRIME*, VOLUME ONE

I'M PRETTY SURE IT'S IMPOSSIBLE TO keep a secret and eat spaghetti at the same time, because I just picked at my food at dinner that Friday night. Thankfully, Mom was rushing out the door to meet the lawyer, so us guys took our bowls to the living room to watch TV. I pretended to watch the news, where the announcer told us about some terrorist group in Europe, but all I could think about was my promise to the government. And watching bad guys on TV was not helpful.

Stark and Fullerton had left, promising to come up with a way to get my parents to sign off on this whole secret agent thing. I didn't sleep a wink that night.

So when the phone rang, waking me from a good nap late Saturday morning, I expected it to be Agent Fullerton. I let Dad answer it and waited. A few minutes later, he knocked on my bedroom door.

"Your mother called," he said, frowning at my reading progress of three pages on *The History of Crime*. "There's been a change of plans. We're meeting with the principal in an hour."

So this wasn't the government calling after all. "At school, on a Saturday?"

"Guess so, champ." Dad shrugged.

I closed my book. "Why not Monday?"

"Something about a new deal." Dad looked at me. "For you."

I'm pretty sure Principal Thornton has a script for his speeches, since they usually follow a standard three-act format.

Everyone sits, and we all take a moment to feel uncomfortable about being there.

Principal Thornton drones on about character, responsibility, and the "gravity of the situation."

I apologize about six times. He gives me detention.

So I was all ready for the usual on Saturday morning,

especially once Thornton showed his pearly whites. "I'm glad you could come in today, Mr. and Mrs. Baker."

My mom sat with her legs crossed. She was in her scrubs, since she had a shift at the hospital later. She said, "You mentioned on the phone that you had some urgent things to discuss about Linc's trouble. Something about an arrangement?" Mom liked to get to the point.

Principal Thornton didn't. He had his script to follow, after all. "You have to understand the gravity of the situation," he said slowly.

"We do," Mom said. Dad just sat back in his chair.

"Lincoln here caused a lot of trouble during yesterday's school expedition," Principal Thornton went on, ignoring Mom. He made a little tent with his fingers. "This isn't the first time Lincoln here has caused damages for the school. Damages that I, as principal, have to account for. Make right, if you will."

I was pretty sure Dad was sleeping with his eyes open. Mom looked like she was about to clock Principal Thornton.

"Farmer Johnson is suing Lompoc Middle School. Lincoln here is no longer welcome. He's being expelled."

"*Expelled*? I thought he was just being suspended. Lincoln is ready to make amends," Mom argued.

I wanted to tell them both that I was sitting right there and that they could talk to me, instead of *about* me. But it was best to keep my mouth shut, I knew from previous meetings with Principal Thornton. The phone rang, and the principal answered. "Send him in," he said.

That was when Agent Fullerton showed up. Instead of his black suit from last night, he wore a navy sports coat, jeans, and a white polo shirt. He looked like the boss of something. "Hello." He shook Mom's and Dad's hands, ignoring me completely. Flashing an expensive-looking golden watch, he introduced himself as Ned Fullerton, head of Fresh Start Incorporated, a company running camps for kids.

"Fresh Start Incorporated?" Mom asked. She was not impressed by Agent Fullerton. "What does this have to do with Lincoln?"

Dad obviously bought the whole act. "What kind of camp is this?" he asked.

Agent Fullerton smiled. "It's a camp for troubled kids. Kids who might need a little more discipline. It's boot camp designed to change Lincoln into an improved version of himself."

A version called Benjamin Green, I thought.

"We can give Lincoln all the discipline he needs at home," Mom shot back. I'd warned Agent Fullerton that she would be toughest to convince. Mom liked to have me home, eating apples and yogurt, and doing my math homework. "A boot camp! Like they do with soldiers?"

"Not exactly," Agent Fullerton answered. He had this fake, reassuring voice. "Like our company name says: we give kids a fresh start. This camp is especially designed to teach Lincoln here how to make better choices, how to control impulses, like opening up chicken cages."

I was pretty sure Mom was buying into it now, too, but

she still shook her head. "No. Linc's staying home."

"When he gets back, he'll be able to attend Lompoc Middle School again, no expulsion," Agent Fullerton said with his eyes on the principal. Principal Thornton gave a curt nod. You could tell Thornton wasn't looking forward to having me back at any time, not even after some super-duper boot camp. "This sort of preemptive correction of behavior also looks good when it comes time to go to court."

"Where is this camp, exactly?" Dad sat up.

"George." Mom grabbed his arm. "We're not sending our twelve-year-old son to boot camp. I don't care about any lawsuit." Mom didn't sound convincing at all.

Dad put his hand over hers. "Where?"

"It's top secret, sir," Agent Fullerton said, pretending to be sorry for not being able to tell them where I was going. "It's a secluded but safe facility—that's all I can say. It's been our experience that it's better if parents don't know."

Dad nodded. "Of course."

"I'm glad to hear we'll have Lincoln here join our boot camp." Agent Fullerton clapped his hands like it was in the bag.

"No," Mom said again. She pulled her hand away from Dad's. "Linc's not going."

5

SATURDAY, NOON.

AGENT FULLERTON LOOKED LOST. WHICH

was when I figured it was time for Lincoln here (that would be me) to speak. This was my chance to change things for my family and make up for all the trouble I'd caused. I owed Mom and Dad that. Plus, I'd made a deal with Fullerton, so now I had to step up. "I want to go, Mom."

Mom looked at me, horrified. "Really? It's boot camp, Linc."

"I know." I looked at the principal, Dad, and back at Mom again. It was time to tell them what they wanted to hear. "I've got to change, Mom. I know I make bad decisions and that I always cause trouble even when I don't mean to. Maybe this camp is just what I need."

Mom just stared at me, her mouth gaping a little.

"It's just like being grounded, but I'll be somewhere else. So you and Dad don't have to worry about me. And it might make this lawsuit go away." I gave Agent Fullerton a stare, and he gave me a tiny nod, confirming our deal.

Mom closed her mouth, then slumped in her seat a little. "Boot camp?" she mumbled.

"It's okay, Mom." I gave her my most convincing smile, like I was oh so happy to go.

She still took what seemed like forever before finally agreeing. "Okay. If this is what Linc wants, I'll go along with it." Mom sat up and looked at Agent Fullerton in that way she always does when I'm supposed to clean my room or something like that. "But he calls me. Every day."

"I don't think—"

"Or he's not going."

Agent Fullerton nodded. "I think we can arrange that."

The adults were practically high-fiving one another over this whole boot camp plan, and I went back to being "Lincoln here." Mom gave Agent Fullerton her speech about nutrition and the growing child, and Dad somehow ended up talking about tire tread with Principal Thornton. They were relieved.

Meanwhile, I was sweating bullets. Thinking of this exchange, these bad dudes, and where they made Benjamin Green disappear to. It was a good thing my parents had no idea what they were really signing me up for.

We left the principal's office. Agent Fullerton followed

us home in his dark sedan. I was supposed to gather some essentials and leave with him for boot camp right away.

I was stuffing an extra sweater in my backpack when Dad knocked on my bedroom door. Even though it was open. "Hey, Linc."

"Hey, Dad."

"All set and ready to go?" He pointed at my backpack.

I nodded. This was weird. I'd been away on overnight trips before, once with school, but never longer than a night or two. "You think I can bring my skateboard?"

"Why not?" Dad said, sounding a little distracted. He looked me in the eye. "You sure you're ready, Linc?"

"Yeah." Not really, but this wasn't the time to be wimping out. "It'll be good for me."

Dad smiled. "I hope so, buddy." He took his keys and moved them around the ring. "Here." He unhooked the small metal compass and put it in my palm.

"But isn't this yours, from Grandpa?"

"And now it's yours. My Boy Scout days are long over anyways." He wrapped my fingers around it and patted my fist. "Remember, home is west."

"Depending on where you are."

He laughed. "Yeah."

I clipped the compass to the loop on my backpack, feeling very sad all of a sudden. I really just wanted to stay here with Dad at Baker Autos, changing the oil on some clunker.

"Time to go." Agent Fullerton stood in the doorway, tapping his gold watch. I took my backpack and skateboard, and everyone followed me outside to Agent Fullerton's parked car. Mom hugged me and I had to repeat our home number like I was five years old. Dad patted me on the shoulder all father-to-son like. I got in a car with Agent Fullerton, and I was on my own.

As I waved to my parents and watched my house disappear behind the trees that lined the sidewalk I skateboarded on to school every day, I felt really scared for the first time in years.

"Where *are* we going?" I asked Agent Fullerton as he turned onto the main street out of Lompoc. "You can tell me. My parents aren't around."

"We're headed toward Los Angeles, to the Ventura Hacienda Hotel. You'll be trained to take Benjamin Green's place in the field."

"Okay. So this Benjamin Green guy, he's a kid my age? And a secret agent?" I was trying to make sense of it all.

"Yes and yes. Benjamin Green is one of our first junior agents." Fullerton sounded kind of proud of this, like maybe he came up with the whole idea. "Only the country's finest make it into the junior agent training program."

"Wait—you have a training camp for kids?"

Agent Fullerton nodded. "Our government got intel a few years ago that the Chinese and the Russians were using kids in their undercover ops and that they have training camps. So naturally, we had to have some, too."

"Naturally." Undercover kid agents? The world governments had gone nuts.

"Normally, our junior agents only work on low-risk cases—crimes in middle schools and high schools, that sort of thing. We found the infiltration of junior agents to be very helpful in solving crime. You kids can go places and be unnoticed in ways our adult agents can't."

"So what was Ben doing?"

"We'll brief you on Monday," Fullerton said.

"So this is what's in Los Angeles—a junior agent boot camp I have to go to?"

"No," Agent Fullerton said with a little laugh. "It takes months, *years* to train an agent. Especially you kids. The vetting process alone takes almost a year." He shook his head. "There's no time to turn you into a *real* junior agent, especially not one of Benjamin Green's caliber. Luckily, you need to be Benjamin Green just for a day—an hour!"

At this point, Agent Fullerton started telling me all about this fantastic Benjamin Green. How he had a black belt in karate and could run five miles at Olympic record speed. How he knew Mandarin (apparently, that's Chinese), aced every test at school, and could lift a hundred pounds with his pinkie.

All right, so I made that last part up, but you get the idea. The guy was a superhero, and I was Linc the Chicken Boy. By the time we exited the freeway just north of LA, I hated Benjamin Green.

"How can a kid know all that?" I asked at the end of Agent Fullerton's speech.

"Benjamin Green applies himself," Agent Fullerton said,

like it was an accusation. "Failure isn't an option for him."

This guy really knew how to make you feel special. "I'm athletic, sort of," I argued, not liking being called a loser. "I played baseball for a while—I was a great pitcher."

"Until you quit." Agent Fullerton smirked. "You're one of those kids who's always looking for an easy way out. You never finish what you start."

"That's not true," I muttered, but he had a point, or at least a little bit of a point, anyway.

"So now you get a chance to be a real hero."

By pretending to be Benjamin Green. This was not cheering me up at all.

That was, until I saw our accommodations. You know those fancy hotels, the ones with the giant pool, the big rooms with fluffy white towels, and the bellhop in the lobby, ready to take your luggage to your room? The Ventura Hacienda was one of those. It was right on the beach, and as we drove up, I got a glimpse of the pool in the back. I'd always dreamed of staying in a hotel like the Ventura Hacienda, and, as you may have guessed, my family was on a discount-motel budget. So I probably got out of the car just a little too fast.

"This isn't a vacation," Agent Fullerton said. "You're here to work, and that's it. So you can forget about that pool and the beach."

That would be difficult. But then Agent Stark met us in the shiny, Spanish-tiled lobby, looking crankier than yesterday. There was a blue folder tucked under her arm. At the far end of the lobby, there was a wall of high glass windows and French doors, and I could see the big blue pool. There for me not to enjoy.

Agent Fullerton slapped me on the back. "I'll see you Monday."

"Wait—you're not staying?"

"Agent Fullerton is needed in the field," Agent Stark said as he walked away. "I'll be getting you ready."

"You sound really happy about that," I said.

"Come on. I'll show you to your room."

6

SATURDAY, 2 P.M.

"YOU'RE IN ROOM 405." AGENT STARK
swiped the key card. For all the fancy exterior of the Ventura
Hacienda, my room looked a lot like the ones in the motels
my family had stayed in before, surprisingly. Agent Stark
pointed at a door in the corner. "I'm on the other side of that
door, room 406."

"Like a babysitter," I said, but to be honest, I kind of liked
the idea of having someone I knew nearby.

"Read this." Agent Stark handed me the blue folder
she'd been carrying around. It had a yellow sticker on it:
CLASSIFIED. There was a pocket-size army-green book with
black letters: *Junior Agent Manual*. And she tossed a couple

of DVD cases, plastered with more CLASSIFIED stickers, on the bed. This was going to be fun, I could tell already. "Research. Get to work." She grabbed my backpack.

"Hey, that's mine!"

"You'll get it back." Agent Stark's tone told me there was no room for negotiation. "I'm going out, but I should return by six."

"Out? Where?"

"Don't worry about what I'm doing," Agent Stark said as she opened the door. "Just worry about what you need to do. I'll be back."

The door closed, and it was really quiet all of a sudden. I sat down on the bed, opened the folder, and saw a registration form of some kind. It had Benjamin Green's name at the top and a photo that looked like a mug shot. It was very creepy, like looking at myself, only his eyes were different. Cold. The form had his height, weight, and hair color (same as me, only he had a blond streak). A bunch of words were covered in black bars, like someone had used a Sharpie. I tried to see if I could read what was underneath, but no luck.

I flipped through the pages. More government forms with boxes and tiny letters, lots more blacked out. Pages and pages of it—at least fifty sheets of boring were waiting for me. And all the quiet was making me itchy, so I decided to call home on the hotel phone.

"Mom?"

"Hi, Lincoln. How's camp?"

"Good. Real good. Is Dad around?" I asked, changing the subject.

"He's off to your uncle's to practice. He has a job interview at Meineke Monday morning."

"Meineke?" I was about to ask why but didn't really have to. It was my fault. Business had been dropping at the shop ever since the tomato incident, and now the family was getting sued.

"He pulled a few favors, and it looks like he'll be able to work a part-time shift. Just until things pick back up at the shop and the lawsuit is done." She sounded nervous.

I ached inside as I pictured my dad interviewing at Meineke, wearing his only suit. "How are things going with the lawsuit?" I asked.

"Don't you worry about that." That was Mom-speak for not good.

"How bad is it?" I felt my throat tighten.

"Farmer Johnson is suing us for a million dollars." Mom exhaled the number, like it sucked the breath from her lungs. "He claims lost earnings, pain and suffering, slander."

"Might as well be a billion," I mumbled.

"We'll figure this out, Linc. We always do. I have to head to work now. You just keep your chin up, okay?"

I felt like I was going to cry like a baby, so I bit my lip. "Okay, Mom. Tell Dad I said hi." After I hung up, I sat holding the phone. Realizing I'd managed to mess up everyone's life by letting a bunch of chickens out of a barn, I felt myself get angry. But I wasn't angry with Agent Stark or Fullerton, or with super junior agent Benjamin Green—even if they were making my life miserable.

I was angry at me.

I was the one who'd been stupid, picking a food fight, setting off that Code Adam alert, opening chicken cages—what was I thinking? I punched the pillows behind me and sat up a little more, determined to focus on Benjamin Green. I would study.

I opened up the blue file. Benjamin Green grew up in Virginia, with both his parents (Rhonda and Jon) in the CIA. I could just imagine the convo at that dinner table. Or maybe since everything in their lives was classified, there wasn't any talking at all.

Now, I know you must be bored with this guy already—I know I was. I'll give you a quick recap so we can get to the part where I get my first taste of junior agent life and things get interesting. Here's what I learned about Benjamin Green:

He started boot camp the week of his twelfth birthday.

He's an expert at everything: archery, track—he even speaks German and French, and aced history, economics, and foreign politics.

He's lactose intolerant (maybe his enemy could kill him with milk?).

Imagine if you got a glimpse at a robotlike super version of yourself. You'd feel like a loser, right? That's how I felt for sure.

So I tossed the file aside. TV was more my style anyway.

The hotel had a decent-sized flat screen TV setup, and I popped in the DVD. It seemed like some kind of training video, because there were these buzzwords that popped up every once in a while.

Focus. Commitment. Dedication.

I rolled my eyes. There was Benjamin Green, of course, at junior agent training camp, the successful graduate showing a scrawny-looking redheaded boy how to do a push-up. Next, he timed the same redheaded kid with a stopwatch, shaking his head because the kid wasn't going fast enough. And later, he showed some girl how to read a map. Then he shook her hand, like the rock star he was.

I yawned. My lousy night's sleep was catching up with me. And, as hard as I tried, my eyes just didn't seem to focus. I dozed off into a deep sleep, the kind that makes you drool on your pillow.

I dreamed of sunshine, the rays dancing on the pool waves, making it hard to see. I was in my regular clothes, but for some reason, I thought it was a good idea to swim. I was underwater, happy, enjoying the nice quiet, until I saw a pair of angry eyes. Brown hair in a ponytail, dangling above me.

And I got another splash of cold water on my face.

"Hey!"

"Wake up!" Agent Stark pulled away. "You're supposed to be studying."

I wiped away the water. "I was studying. But the movie was boring, and all those blacked-out parts in the files were making my eyes glaze over."

"That's the top secret stuff they blacked out for you."

"Very helpful."

"Here." Agent Stark dropped two big shopping bags on the bed. She rolled a new suitcase into a corner.

I pulled two pairs of black cargo pants, black polo shirts, and a knitted black pullover out of the bags. "Am I joining the goth squad? In case you haven't noticed, I'm not color-blind." I pointed at my more colorful California garb.

Agent Stark looked me in the eyes. "Who are you?"

I knew what she wanted me to say, but instead I extended my hand with a smile. "Lincoln Baker, pleased to meet you."

She sighed. "We have a long way to go." Agent Stark dug inside one of the bags and pulled out a box of hair dye. There was a pretty lady on the front with white streaks in her hair—she looked like a zebra, to tell you the truth. "Come on. We can at least make you look like Benjamin Green."

It wasn't until I followed her to the bathroom that I got it. "The blond streak."

"That's right." Agent Stark opened the box and mixed some powder with liquid until the whole place reeked.

"You're not going to put this on my head, are you?"

Agent Stark looked at me, squinting a little from the strong chemical smell. "This is dangerous business. If you have any doubts, now's the time to bow out, Linc. Once we put this junk in your hair and we send you into the field, there's no going back."

"I get it." I thought of Dad, in his nice suit, applying for a job at Meineke—because of me. "I'm in, okay?"

She stepped even closer, and given that we were in the bathroom, that was close enough for me to smell the coffee on her breath. "Do you get how important this is? You were napping on top of your research material, Lincoln."

"It's Benjamin," I said, looking at myself in the mirror. "I'm Benjamin Green." Then I said something that I never thought I would ever say in my life. "Let's color my hair."

7

PLACE: VENTURA HACIENDA HOTEL

TIME: SUNDAY, 6 A.M.

STATUS: SLEEPING IN A FLUFFY BED

A LOUD BANGING ON MY DOOR HAD ME jumping out of bed the next morning.

"Wake up!" a voice shouted. More banging on my door.

I looked at my clock—6 a.m. What idiot was waking me this early? Sundays were for sleeping in, everybody knew that. "Who is it?"

No answer.

I rubbed my head, spreading the smell of peroxide around. I remembered: the streak in my hair and how I really looked like Benjamin Green now. I walked to the door and looked out the peephole, but saw nothing. More banging, making me jump since I was right at the door. I strained to look down and saw a mop of red hair. There was a redheaded kid banging on my door at 6 a.m.

"Time for your run, Benjamin Green."

And then I got it: this kid was here as part of the mission somehow. He thought I was Benjamin Green, and I was supposed to go for a run.

I opened the door and looked down at a scrawny kid, a good inch shorter and at least twenty pounds lighter than me. He wore a blue sweat suit with some crest on it, and had freckles all over his face, even on his wrist, I noticed as he extended his hand to shake mine. "Henry, Martin Henry. But you can call me Henry—everyone does except my mom." I knew who he was: that redheaded kid from the DVD, the one getting push-up pointers from Benjamin Green. Henry grinned. "Gosh, this really is kind of an honor."

"Right." I blinked, still waking up a little. "So you're still in junior agent training, right?"

He laughed. "Gosh, I just can't believe they let me— me!—come out here to join this mission with you."

So this Henry was another kid in Pandora. "What are you, my partner?"

"No." Henry shook his head. "I'm the tech guy."

"Ah." It was too early for me to wonder why there would be a need for one.

Henry grinned. "You're, like, my hero."

"I know," I grumbled. Then I remembered I was Ben. I brushed my hair back like he did in the video, feeling weird. "I'm flattered, Henry, but I'm sure I can skip the ol' six a.m. run for a day."

"Agent Stark told me you might say that. She said you've been slacking on your training a little. That's so unlike you." Another wide grin. "She also said you might try to bribe me to get out of running."

So much for my plan B.

"Come on," Henry said. "You can beat me at the five k like you did at training camp, Ben."

I swallowed. "Okay. Just let me change into my gym gear." At this point, I seriously considered crawling back in bed and leaving Henry out there. But I knew he wouldn't leave, so I dug around in the shopping bags of Ben stuff to find a tracksuit and sneakers.

I sounded like a walking tent as I followed Henry down to a deserted lobby, outside to the big deck with pool, and down the steps to a chilly beach. "Race ya," he said, and started kicking up sand.

I should probably mention right now that I qualify for the *Guinness Book of World Records* as the slowest, most out-of-shape twelve-year-old in history. By the time I reached the surf, I thought I was going to die. Henry was far ahead of me, running like that's all he ever did, his legs moving faster than I'd ever seen anyone's move.

And I was supposed to be Benjamin Green, super junior agent! I stopped running and leaned my hands on my knees.

My lungs were on fire. Up ahead of me, Henry turned around and stopped. To gloat, no doubt.

I gave him a little wave, then thumbed over my shoulder to the hotel. I was only supposed to be Benjamin Green for this exchange, for an hour, Agent Fullerton said. I didn't need to be an Olympic athlete for that. I was going back upstairs to catch up on my sleep.

But then I saw Henry. He looked panicked, running back in my direction even faster than I'd seen him run already.

Was my hair on fire or something? Was the hotel blowing up? I looked over my shoulder. Behind, there was the Ventura Hacienda, looking fancy as ever. Some guy was cleaning the pool, and another one was sweeping the deck. A lady in a jogging suit was tying her shoes, one foot propped on a patio chair, her back toward me.

Henry raced up. "You have a tail!" he hissed, pulling me along.

"A what?" I almost looked back at my behind to see what he was talking about—but then I got it.

Someone was following me.

"You're the rabbit, I shoulda known," Henry mumbled. "Come on." He clenched his teeth and made his way toward the hotel. I was a bunny? I didn't think so. But I followed him anyway, curious now. Who did he think was following me?

We reached the giant hotel deck and Henry stopped, like he wasn't sure what to do. Guy One was still sweeping the deck—the same spot, I was pretty sure. Guy Two was lazily combing the net through the pool. They looked like they were working very hard at not working. But Henry obviously saw something else. He squinted, pointed at me, and then at Guy One.

Before I even understood what was going on, Henry sprinted toward him. With a low karate-type kick, Henry looped his right leg in front of the guy's legs and swooped them out from under him. And Guy One landed in the pool with a splash, still clutching the broom.

Then Henry sprinted toward the guy with the pool net and shoved him. Hard. Sending him flying into the pool. The net on a stick clattered on the pool deck.

"Take that, you fools," Henry said with a contented grin.

"Those guys were following me?"

Henry nodded, using the pool cleaning net on a stick like a lance to keep his victims floating in the pool. They looked pretty angry.

But not as miffed as Agent Stark. She ran up from the beach in her jogging suit, stalked onto the deck, and snatched the pool cleaning net from Henry's hand. "What the heck did you do?"

8

SUNDAY, 7 A.M.

AFTER AGENT STARK HELPED THE GUYS

out of the pool, she took us both aside. "Whose idea was it to take down these hotel employees?"

"Mine." Henry waved his hand, looking like he just got an F on his latest homework assignment. Which was probably not that far from the truth. "I left my glasses up in my room, and I'm kinda blind without 'em. Sorry."

"And you?" She gave me her death-ray stare. "Where were you in all of this?"

"Agent Green had nothing to do with this," Henry said before I could. "He is the best, after all."

Agent Stark squinted. "Right."

Henry tried a smile. "We had a great run. Benjamin here

swept the floor with me—look," he said, and raised his arms and shoved his sweaty underarms right under Agent Stark's nose. "I'm drenched."

Agent Stark recoiled at the sight of Henry's soaked pits.

"Agent Green didn't even break a sweat." Henry lowered his arms.

"It's all in the training." I hoped I sounded convincing.

"I'll have to fix things with the hotel now. You recruits wash up. *Benjamin*, I'll catch up with you later."

Henry waited until she was out of earshot before he asked, "Who are you?" He stepped closer and looked me in the eye. "The Benjamin Green I know wouldn't stop running. He'd never pass up a chance to show me he's better, and then he'd throw the *Junior Agent Manual* in my face."

I stepped back. "I just left the manual in my room, that's all."

"You're not Benjamin Green."

"Yes, I am."

"No, you're not."

"Yes, I am." I took another step back. "I'm Benjamin Green." I tried to stand tall, like Ben would, but I knew Henry wasn't buying it.

"You're some kind of fake." Henry nodded and kept smiling with a smug expression on his face. "I knew it!"

I felt my face go red. So much for pulling off this double thing.

"You walk different." Henry stepped closer again. "Oh, and you get embarrassed."

"You got me. I'm Linc Baker," I mumbled, feeling like an idiot. "And I *can* run. I beat lots of kids in PE, you know." Well, some of them anyway.

"No wonder you looked all confused when I called you a rabbit," Henry said with a nod.

"I'm no rabbit."

"Not a *bunny* rabbit." Henry snickered. "Geez, you're really clueless, aren't you? A rabbit is someone who's being followed."

"But nobody was."

"No, I guess not." Henry shrugged, then laughed and poked me in the ribs. "It was fun, back there. Did you see how those guys went flying?"

I laughed. It was funny.

"I call that move 'the Henry,'" Henry said with pride. "You hook the guy from the front by extending your right leg so you can take out both of his legs, so he can only go down." He looped his leg around mine.

"I get it! Henry, stop!"

He stepped away, but you could tell he really liked his move. "I learned in training camp that I can't beat these other guys. I mean, look at me. I'm not strong or athletic, or anything like that. So the key is to be smarter."

"Maybe that's what I need to do: be smarter. I know I can't be Ben. Thanks for covering for me, you know, about me not being Benjamin Green," I said.

"No problem." Henry shrugged. "I hate Benjamin Green,

so I'm actually glad you're not him."

"What? You seemed so excited when you showed up to run this morning."

"That's because I thought you were Ben. I had to pretend to like you."

"You were faking. So why do you hate him?"

"He's perfect, and he knows it." Henry sighed. "He used to be my hero. I'd watch the videos in training camp and see how awesome he was. I wanted to be that great at everything, so I worked really hard to get fit, you know? And then he came to visit training camp, so I was all amped. I was going to meet the great Benjamin Green!" Henry waved his arms.

"What happened?"

"He was on me the whole time. How I wasn't fast enough, strong enough—whatever. And now look: I just took down two guys who weren't even following you." Henry's shoulders slumped. "Agent Fullerton is right: I'm not cut out to be in the field."

"You're doing better than me."

Henry smiled. "Thanks. So what's the story? Who are you, and where's Benjamin Green?"

I told him everything that happened: the chicken farm disaster, the lawsuit, the agents showing up on my porch, and how I was supposed to take Benjamin Green's place during an important exchange because the guy had gone missing. "I have to do this. For my family, for my dad."

Henry nodded. "Look, all you have to learn to do is how

to act like the guy. You have the videos of him?"

I nodded.

"Then you can fake it." He grinned. "I don't know where he is, but as his former greatest fan, I'm the expert on all things Benjamin Green. Come on, I'll help you."

SUNDAY, 9 A.M.

IF THIS WERE A MOVIE, NOW WOULD BE
the part where they play some pumped-up tune, showing me
running, sweating, and learning all about Benjamin Green
while guzzling energy drinks. But as you've probably figured
out by now, this isn't your typical action-hero story. We
guzzled orange juice instead of power drinks and ordered
room service, too: big stacks of pancakes with extra syrup.

Henry perched a plate on his lap as we both sat on the
bed in my hotel room. "You should see what passes as food
at boot camp." He told me his mother was an FBI agent and
his dad some sort of intelligence analyst. Between bites,
he added, "I rewired the intercom system at my school so
everyone could hear the teachers in the teachers' lounge. I

also turned an MP3 player into a minibomb."

"You sound like the kind of guy I want on my team."

Henry grinned. "Lucky for you, I am. I'm your technology expert."

"What's that?"

"Your gadget guy. I invented this thing called the Tickstick."

"The tick *what*?"

"Never mind, you'll see it when we get to Paris."

"I'm going to Paris?"

Henry nodded. "Cool, huh? I already have schematics done up for some really cool tech gear for you. That's how I ended up getting recruited for the Pandora, you know. If it wasn't for my inventions, I'd still be in boot camp." Henry put his empty plate on the room service tray and started the DVD. "You know, for all the running and push-ups we do, the junior agent training camp teaches you one thing that has nothing to do with being fit."

"What's that?"

"Observation skills. Just watch Benjamin Green and how he moves." Henry started the DVD.

First, the training video talked about basic junior agent strategy—know your exit strategy: plan your exit before you start, keep your eye on the enemy, blah, blah. Then there was lots of footage of Benjamin Green at junior agent training camp, criticizing Henry's push-ups. Ben shook his head when he clocked Henry's running time.

"Friendly guy."

Henry shrugged. "He's just . . ."

"Benjamin Green. But I'll bet he doesn't know how to change the oil on a '99 Chevy Blazer. Or how to turn an MP3 player into a minibomb."

Henry paused the DVD, leaving Benjamin Green frozen with his mouth half open. "All right, so let's see your best Benjamin Green," Henry said as he sat up on the bed.

I felt stupid now. "What am I supposed to do?"

"Say something Benjamin Green would say."

"Hi, I'm Benjamin Green."

Henry shook his head. "That's terrible."

"Thanks."

Henry straightened his shoulders and crossed his arms. "That's not a full push-up, recruit," he said in a fake-deep voice, frowning. Henry pushed me. "Now you try."

"That is not—"

"Try a lower tone of voice, like you're more important than everyone else."

I tried again, but it wasn't any good.

"Forget the tone. It's more about *how* you say it." Henry frowned as he thought for a minute. "You have to get your mind into it. Really think you actually are Benjamin Green."

"I don't even know him. In fact, I think I'm the complete opposite of the guy." I laughed.

"That's it!" Henry jumped up.

"What?"

"Think of whatever you would do or say, and do the opposite."

That actually made total sense.

"Now try the voice." Henry sat back down on the bed.

I cleared my throat. "That's not a full push-up, recruit."

"Really good! Now cross your arms and frown." Henry made a serious face, just like Benjamin Green in the video.

"I'm Benjamin Green," I said, crossing my arms and straightening my shoulders. "And I'm the best secret agent in the universe."

"That's so good, it's creepy. Do it again."

I'd like to say I did as well on the Benjamin facts from the files, but I pretty much stank at remembering his hometown, favorite music, and food. Was it broccoli? Something gross and healthy like that—as Henry said: Benjamin Green was perfect.

We practiced all day and even went over some of the *Junior Agent Manual.* Okay, so maybe it was more Henry who read it, not me. We took a break for pizza and some TV. And then we made up facts about the case, since neither one of us knew anything. Except that we were going to Paris. But otherwise, this secret agent training was pretty dull—I mean you're bored just reading this, right?

So I'll fast-forward to the next day: Monday morning, 7 a.m. That's when Agent Fullerton showed up at my hotel room just as I was messing up on Henry's latest who-is-Benjamin-Green quiz. "Time to go," was all Fullerton said.

And that's when things got dangerous. Fast.

10

PLACE: LOS ANGELES INTERNATIONAL AIRPORT

TIME: MONDAY, 10 A.M.

STATUS: READY TO BE BENJAMIN GREEN (SORT OF, ANYWAY)

OKAY, SO MAYBE IT DIDN'T GET DAN-gerous *immediately*. First, we had to pack, then there was a really long cab ride to the airport, and after that we had to go through security—you get the idea. But apparently, being a secret agent means you get to travel in style, because there was a big shiny white private plane waiting for us on the tarmac. Since I didn't have my own passport, I got to take a copy Pandora had done up of Benjamin Green's. He looked really gloomy in the picture.

The Baker family doesn't take vacations, not the kind where you take an airplane, anyway. Our getaways are more the road trip variety, with peanut butter sandwiches and bananas for lunch at a rest stop. So I was pretty excited to fly. As we walked toward the plane, Agent Fullerton starting quizzing me. "What's Benjamin Green's favorite color?"

"Uhm, red?"

"No, it's blue." His face darkened. "Favorite food?"

"Broccoli. No, something else green."

"Spinach."

Yuck. "And a protein shake for breakfast," I blurted out. Happy I remembered something, I took two stairs at a time.

"At least you got that one right." Agent Fullerton followed me into the plane. "What have you been doing these past two days—watching TV?"

"I studied." I just wasn't very good at it.

"It'll have to do." Agent Fullerton motioned to the four seats at the other end of the plane, two sets facing each other, where Agent Stark was talking to Henry. "Let's get both of you briefed on the case."

Agent Stark had managed to set up a projector despite the small space, and had it shining at a tiny fold-down screen. "Henry says you told him you weren't Benjamin Green?"

"Yeah," I said, unsure what the right answer was.

Henry passed me a cold bottle of water, giving me a wink. "I never would have known. Linc is *very* convincing as Benjamin Green."

"Right." Agent Stark adjusted her seat. "So then you know Henry will be your technology expert on this mission."

I nodded.

"Good. As soon as the plane takes off, we'll talk about the case," she said as she turned off the lights.

Soon Agent Stark was clicking to a slide of the *Mona Lisa*, secure behind a glass enclosure. Dozens of people crowded around it, staring at the painting like it held some kind of secret. "As you may know, the *Mona Lisa* hangs in the Louvre Museum in Paris."

"Of course." Henry nodded. I was busy digging in my mental archives—I should've paid better attention in Art History. "Doesn't it have its own room in the museum?"

"That's right," Agent Stark said. "The glass enclosure is bulletproof and controls the temperature and humidity inside to preserve it. The *Mona Lisa* is worth around five hundred million, and is impossible to steal."

I almost spit my water across the plane. "Five hundred million. *Dollars?*"

"Give or take a few million," Agent Fullerton joked. He had been pretty quiet up to now. His eyes lingered on the *Mona Lisa*, like maybe he could suck out the five hundred million that way.

"It was stolen last week," Agent Stark said.

"Wait," I said. "You just told us it's impossible to steal." Already, this operation was making no sense.

"Bear with me." Agent Stark went to the next slide. It

looked like a little store—but then when you looked closer, you could see the basket of French bread in the window, the pastries and cakes on display. "This is Maison du Mégère." Agent Stark pronounced it *Mayson du Meyzere*. "It's a patisserie—a bakery—in the Latin Quarter of Paris, not far from the Louvre. They make bread, pies, pastries, chocolates—it's one of the best bakeries in Paris."

"Does the thief live there?" Henry asked. He was all gung ho to go over to this bakery and take someone down with "the Henry."

Agent Stark let out a little sigh. "No, this is where the *Mona Lisa* was stolen from."

I started laughing, but then I realized agents Stark and Fullerton weren't—they were dead serious.

"Back in the sixteenth century, when Leonardo da Vinci originally painted the *Mona Lisa*, it wasn't uncommon for artists to do a painting twice—make a double, basically. That way, if one got destroyed or stolen, there would be another," Agent Stark said.

Henry started nodding now. "I heard about this. It's an original; there are just two of them, like a twin. Da Vinci did this with some other painting of this lady—"

"*Virgin on the Rocks,*" Agent Stark said, finishing his sentence.

I'll save you the boring parts of this slide show, where Agent Stark was talking about Leonardo da Vinci, his paintings, and how he used this glazing technique, blah,

blah. I zoned out for a while, until she started talking about the night da Vinci had this party to show all his friends the *Mona Lisa*.

Agent Stark's face darkened. "One of the guests said something like, 'Who wouldn't you kill to own this beautiful painting?' Then all of da Vinci's friends looked at the *Mona Lisa*, mesmerized by her eyes, her captivating smile."

"They were hypnotized," Agent Fullerton added.

Agent Stark continued, "How long they stood there, no one knows for sure. But that evening, da Vinci's friends turned into a murderous, crazy mob. Several people died that night."

"Because one of them suggested they should kill?" I asked.

Agent Stark nodded. "This evil *Mona Lisa* has hypnotizing power so strong, it can create mass hypnosis—or like that night, mass murder."

"It's a weapon," Henry whispered, shocked by the story.

"Exactly," said Agent Stark. "Look at this evil *Mona Lisa*, and whoever whispers in your ear at the time has complete control of you. When you consider how many people can gather around a painting . . ."

"Hundreds," I mumbled, feeling a sense of dread. "I'll bet every bad guy in the world wants it."

"Thankfully, Leonardo da Vinci realized this, too, and after that horrible night he boxed the painting and found a safe place for it. He didn't want it to be lost, but he didn't want it to hurt anyone either." Agent Stark clicked back to the slide of the pastry shop. "This is where the evil *Mona Lisa* has been kept, in the storage cellar of the Mégère patisserie."

"Really?" I asked, thinking the shop looked too ordinary.

"Would you ever think to look for it there?" she challenged.

Henry and I both shook our heads.

"Right. It's a very clever hiding place."

We had a bumpy patch of air and jolted around a bit before the plane settled and she clicked to the next picture. It showed a grumpy guy, rushing down a street, his back hunched. His graying wiry hair was all over the place, long and wild, like he'd just stuck his finger in an electrical socket.

"Who's this, Albert Einstein?" I joked.

"Meet Jacques Mégère, the owner of the pastry shop. His family has hidden the evil *Mona Lisa* for generations." Agent Stark paused. "Until a few weeks ago, when both Mégère and the painting went missing."

Agent Stark flipped to another slide. There was a guy in a long coat, slicked back hair, sunglasses—but you couldn't really tell much else. The picture was hazy. "An organization led by a man with the code name Drake kidnapped Mégère. This man is believed to be their leader."

Agent Stark droned on for a while, about intel this and classified reports that, but I'll skip past the boring stuff for you. Here's the short version.

This bad dude Drake sells the evil *Mona Lisa* to some

super-powered European terrorist group for five hundred million dollars. But he doesn't actually have it.

So Drake goes to steal the painting from the bakery—how he knew it was there, no one knows. When he realizes Mégère hid it, Drake kidnaps him instead.

But Mégère isn't talking. Drake needs to deliver the evil *Mona Lisa* by 1 p.m. Thanksgiving Thursday.

"The clock is ticking," Agent Stark said after she went through a few dozen slides. "Before Mégère gives up the location of the evil *Mona Lisa*, we need him back."

Agent Fullerton leaned closer, like someone might overhear. Even though we were on a private plane, I looked around. "We made contact with Drake, and told him we have the evil *Mona Lisa*."

"But you don't." Henry smiled. "Nice bluff."

Agent Stark said, "Benjamin Green was supposed to trade the phony evil *Mona Lisa* for Jacques Mégère in an exchange with Drake. The deal is so big, Drake's coming himself."

"Why Ben?" I asked.

"He's a kid," Fullerton said, like it all made sense.

"They're less likely to shoot him," Henry added as explanation.

Fullerton looked at me. "That's where you come in as our Benjamin Green double."

I felt better already.

Agent Stark turned the projector off. "Your objective is to get Jacques Mégère back. And that's your *only* objective. Once we have him, we'll get him to tell us where the Dangerous Double is, so we can neutralize the threat."

"How do you do that?" Henry asked.

Agent Stark got up. "There's only one way. We destroy the evil *Mona Lisa*."

11

PLACE: CHARLES DE GAULLE AIRPORT (THAT'S IN PARIS)

TIME: TUESDAY, 7 A.M.

STATUS: JETLAGGED

RIGHT AFTER OUR BRIEFING, HENRY WAS whisked away to his lab on the other end of the plane, to invent tech stuff for me to use. Whatever that was. The agents were busy pounding the keys of their laptops or talking on the phone. The only thing I had to keep me busy was a classified file of Ben facts with funky-tasting lasagna and a turkey sandwich for dinner or lunch, depending on the time zone you chose.

Sometime during the flight, I used the phone in the armrest to call home so I could hear a friendly voice. But instead, I got Grandpa.

"Where are Mom and Dad?" I asked.

"You're mom's at work, and I think George is working on his shop finances. Listen, Linc, do you know how to turn the answering machine off? There's this fellow with that lawyer's office, whatsit—"

"Zachary Quinn."

"I know his name," Grandpa snapped. "He's been calling about our bank statements or some such, and I'm tired of hearing about it."

"Just hit the off button, Grandpa."

"Okay." And he hung up on me.

After my call, I tried to nap, but all I could think about was evil paintings, Zachary Quinn, and this bad guy Drake.

What if Jacques Mégère caved and told him where the painting was?

And how bad was this guy Drake, exactly? Would he believe I was Benjamin Green at the exchange? What was going on at home with the lawsuit—now this lawyer wanted to see how much money Mom and Dad have? Definitely not a million bucks.

By the time we landed at Charles de Gaulle airport in Paris that Tuesday morning, we'd been on the plane for over ten hours, and I was tired. Henry and Agent Fullerton left together so they could clear customs with Henry's gear and move his lab to the hotel. I got stuck with Agent Stark.

"Change your watch," Agent Stark said as she fixed hers while we waited in line at customs. "It's seven a.m., Tuesday. "

"Wait—we lost a day?" I adjusted my watch. "What a rip-off."

"Welcome to international travel."

Lights in the arrival hall were way too bright. People were rushing everywhere, and they didn't seem one bit concerned about pushing me out of the way. Some kid in a hooded sweatshirt bumped into me without even apologizing. I turned to say something, but he took off too fast.

Agent Stark rushed down the airport hall to get outside. The November wind was cold, especially when you consider that I'm a California kid. I was about to dig into my suitcase of Ben stuff for an extra sweater when a taxi drove straight for me. I jumped out of the way. "Hey, now," I said, too tired to yell.

The black taxi came to an abrupt stop, parked all crooked. "Bonjour!" A tall skinny man with a big nose got out of the small car. If it weren't for the *Taxi Parisienne* sign on the roof, I wouldn't have guessed it was a cab. "You need a taxi?"

"Yes," Agent Stark said.

The cabdriver spread his arms and smiled big. "Welcome to Paris," he said in a heavy French accent. "Where you go, I take you."

Heaven help us. But he was already unloading our bags from the cart.

"Young lady, you do not work, you sit." He guided Agent Stark to the cramped backseat of the cab before she could object. Then he loaded the heavy bags into the small trunk like they were nothing, and pushed my suitcase down hard to make it all fit.

"Get in, get in." He waved me toward the passenger door. I spotted a tattoo of a red and yellow flame on his wrist.

"I am Guillaume," our cabdriver said once I got seated. He popped the cab in reverse and pulled back without looking.

Agent Stark cringed and checked my seat belt, then her own.

Horns blared all around us. Guillaume rolled down his window and yelled something in French I couldn't understand, but I was pretty sure involved cursing. "Paris traffic, right?" He drove away slowly, making the other cars pass us. "What is your hotel?"

"The Princesse," Agent Stark yelled. "Do you know where that is?"

"I know Paris like it is my garden," Guillaume said with a big grin. I assumed he meant he knew it like it was his backyard.

He was driving painfully slow, occasionally asking a nonresponsive Agent Stark questions about where she was from and whether she was on vacation. Meanwhile, I tried my best to see some of Paris. Let's face it: the odds of me ever making it back to Europe were close to zilch. I had to take it in while I could.

The buildings were tall—three, four floors high— and often close together. I was used to California, where everything was spread out and horizontal. The trees were in winter mode, no leaves.

If only my family had come to enjoy it with me. Dad would've loved all the history. Mom would've loved the cafés, the cute shops with awnings. And Grandpa would—well, he'd probably just mope around most of the time, but I knew he'd get a kick out of being in Paris.

I looked out the back window and saw a compact red sedan behind us that zoomed past traffic on the shoulder. It was too far back for me to see in the car, but whoever they were, they were driving like lunatics. I nudged Agent Stark. "Is this guy following us?"

She turned, but just then, the sedan merged with traffic. "I don't see anything." Agent Stark sat back in her seat. "Paris traffic is probably not like what you're used to."

She had a point. Lompoc was a quiet place, with mostly farmers and slow-moving school buses on their way to chicken farms for field trips. Maybe. But then I saw it again: the red sedan, moving around another car to get closer. I was about to tell Agent Stark, when it disappeared from my sight.

Meanwhile, I tried to pay attention to the city. Everything seemed old and grand, like you were supposed to wear a tuxedo just to see the sights. Even the trees along the street were perfectly round and evenly spaced. I was pretty sure that was the Eiffel Tower off in the distance—

But there was the sedan again! I watched it zoom past traffic using the sidewalk, making pedestrians jump aside so they wouldn't get hit. "This red car is definitely following us!"

Agent Stark glanced behind us with a hugely irritated look on her face, but then she saw the red sedan, too. I could tell there were two dark figures in the front, but not much else. "You're right," she mumbled to me. Then to Guillaume, "Can you go any faster?"

Guillaume grinned. "Faster? Of course I can." He slammed the gas pedal and simultaneously yanked the steering wheel. We were on the sidewalk, too.

Then with a sharp left, he took an alleyway, making us bounce on the cobblestones. The alley was so narrow, it was a miracle Guillaume didn't lose his side mirrors.

A sharp turn made the tires squeal, and I was pretty sure we tipped onto the two right wheels for a second there.

"Who *are* those guys?" I asked Agent Stark. But before she could answer, I saw the flash of red behind us. Guillaume must've seen it, too, because he revved the engine. He drove through someone's clothesline, sending a blue shirt and a pair of men's white underwear flying over the windshield.

I thought we were flying, faster and faster, until we headed straight for a giant building.

We were going to crash!

12

TUESDAY, 8 A.M.

GUILLAUME SLAMMED THE BRAKES, missing the building in front of us by no more than a hair. "And here we are," he said as the car skidded to a stop, making me glad I was wearing a seat belt. There was a tall wooden door in front of us. The fancy golden sign dangling to the side—*La Princesse*—told us we'd arrived.

I looked down the larger thoroughfare that was just to the right of the hotel. But no red sedan. Guillaume had managed to lose those guys, whoever they were.

Agent Stark looked very pale as she got out. "Well, thank you, Mr. Guillaume."

"No problem." Guillaume smiled as he unloaded our bags. "Paris traffic, it's a little wild, right?"

Agent Stark nodded, paid him, and took his business card. "Thank you again." She was scanning the roads, too, but there was no red sedan. We were safe.

Guillaume handed me a card, too, which was weird, me being a kid and all. "You need a driver, you call me, okay?" He flashed me a smile. "I'll help you anytime."

I tucked his card in my pants pocket. "Thanks." And he was off, leaving a trail of cranky drivers behind. I looked up to find Agent Stark propping the door open for me. "Come on."

"Who do you think those guys in the red sedan were?" I asked as we went inside.

"Don't worry about that," Agent Stark snapped. "We'll handle it."

The lobby was small and dark, and the lady behind the counter smiled when she saw us come in.

"Hi, I'm Benjamin Green," I said, using my serious Ben voice.

"But of course you are." The lady looked at me like I was her best friend. "It is always good to see you, Monsieur Benjamin."

"Just wait over there while I get the keys and have them take care of our bags," Agent Stark said, gently pushing me aside.

"Are you enjoying your stay?" the receptionist lady asked, like I was her favorite guest. I thought I could get used to the special treatment.

Inside the elevator, Agent Stark swiped her room key

card and punched the P button.

"Only Pandora agents can get to the Penthouse," she said, handing me my room key card. "If you need to come up, just use this."

"We're going to the Penthouse now?"

Agent Stark nodded. "Henry is waiting for you with your gear. We're running behind schedule." It figured that she was one of those people who hate being late. Me, I get there when I can, but now that I was Ben, I was probably going to have to watch the clock.

The elevator did its little ding, and the doors opened right into the penthouse. It looked huge, almost as big as the Lompoc Middle School gym. A big guy in a Hawaiian shirt motioned for Agent Stark to join him as he walked down a hallway, so off she went. I wasn't introduced, and just stood there glancing around at the near-empty room. Dining chairs were stacked against the wall next to the elevator, leaving only a sitting area and a really long dining table with a flat square box on it. "Hey, Linc, you made it!" Henry got up from behind the dining table.

"Like I wouldn't?"

"Come on," Henry said, motioning me to join him. Behind the box, he had a big black backpack—*my* old backpack. With Dad's compass still attached to the loop.

The fabric looked cleaner. "What did you do to it?"

"Check this out." He reached inside the pack and pulled out a device that looked like a phone, along with a small, black plastic box. He pushed the red button on the side of the device, and it lit up. "This is a tracking device." The screen showed a map, with a bunch of red dots clustered together. Henry handed it to me.

"What am I supposed to do with this?" I asked, looking at the red dots. They weren't moving.

"Just wait," Henry said with a glint in his eye. He opened the small plastic box and took out a stack of—

"Stickers?" They had little Eiffel Towers on them and said: J'aime Paris. I guessed that means *I Love Paris*.

"Not just any stickers." Henry took one, and ran across the penthouse hotel room. "Is it moving?" he called from another room.

I looked at the red dots. "Not really." But then one of the dots slid away from the others. "Wait, is that you?"

"Yup." Henry walked back, grinning big. "Cool, right? There's a tracking mechanism in there, so thin, I was able to work it into a sticker." He took the other stickers and put them back in the box. "I only had time to make three, so don't go crazy out there."

"I promise to control my sticker frenzy."

Henry took the tracking device, turned it off, and slid it into the backpack, along with the plastic box of stickers. I wasn't sure who I was supposed to track with those, but then it couldn't hurt, right? Henry pulled out another device, which looked suspiciously like a simple voice recorder I'd seen Mom use for schoolwork. "Say something," he said, pointing the thing in my face.

"Uhm, hello?" I pulled away and heard the recorder spit

out in a fancy lady's voice, "*Bonjour*?"

"It's a translator," Henry said, all excited. "It translates stuff from English to French."

I took the recorder, which was pretty light. "You made this?"

Henry waved dismissively. "No need, you can buy these things off the internet. It comes with earbuds, in case you don't want everyone else to hear what it translates." He handed me a cheap set of buds, like the kind that came with my MP3 player. "Oh, one more thing: the battery life on this thing is terrible. So don't keep it running unless you really need it."

"I'll remember that."

Henry turned off the translator and tucked it into my backpack. "Most people in Paris speak English, so you probably won't need it a lot."

Next, Henry pulled a container that looked like a tube of lip balm out of the front pocket. "Now this is really cool. I call it the Tickstick." He put the container, which looked very ordinary, between his thumb and index finger. "See that seal?" He carefully moved the Tickstick until it was just inches away from my face. There was a sticker taped over the cap, to seal it, like when you bought one new at a store.

"Yeah, I see it."

"When you twist the cap and break the seal," he whispered, looking right into my eyes, pausing dramatically, "BOOM!"

I jumped.

Henry relaxed and put the Tickstick back into the little front zipper pocket. "Well, not until ten seconds later anyway. So you have to run once you twist the cap."

I wiped my sweaty palms on my pants. This junior agent gear was beginning to worry me a little.

"That's why I call it the Tickstick, see? It ticks like a bomb but looks like a lip balm." Henry looked proud.

"Very smart."

"Just don't go blowing up the Eiffel Tower, all right?"

"I'll try not to. I mean, it's not like I'll actually *need* any of this, right?"

Henry didn't answer but just zipped up the backpack. And handed it to me. "Agent Stark had me build in a parachute. You have to open this flap." He pulled a flap of fabric to the side of the pack, exposing a red cord. "Pull this really hard. You should probably only do that if you're, like, really high up in the air."

"You think?"

He reached under the big table and pulled out my skateboard—*my* skateboard! The one I rode to get to school, to Daryl's house, to anywhere. "Agent Stark told me you liked your skateboard. So I created a way to carry it with you, see?" Henry quickly fastened a Velcro strap around the board, attaching it to the backpack, wheels out. "Now you can take it everywhere."

I took the backpack from Henry, surprised by how heavy it felt. "Thanks, Henry."

"I wish I was coming with you," Henry said.

"No, you don't."

"You're right. I'm actually looking forward to getting you some more gadgets." He did look very happy. "Go kick some Drake butt. Get this Jacques Mégère back. Save your family from legal battles. Save the world."

I was about to tell him I wasn't ready, and I had no idea what I was doing, when Agent Stark showed up. "Time to go."

"Where?"

"To the meeting place for the exchange. It's time for you to be Benjamin Green."

13

TUESDAY, 11 A.M.

AGENT STARK GRABBED THE FLAT BOX and we took the elevator, leaving Henry to tinker with his next gadget. Once the doors closed, she showed me a map with an X on it, south of a bridge. "This is where you're meeting: the Pont Neuf. It's a big tourist spot. We chose it so you'd be in a safe, public place. You have an hour to get there, which should be plenty of time."

"Right to work, huh?" No after-airplane naps for me. "Okay." I reached to grab the map, but Agent Stark shook her head. "What, is this classified?" I asked.

"Benjamin Green was trained to know Paris, so Drake will expect you to know your way."

"Of course. But I don't."

"A good agent can memorize a map." Agent Stark's shoulders slumped. "Just try, okay? The cab will drop you nearby, but you'll need to walk this street to get there." She tapped the map with her index finger. "The meeting point is on the bridge, but keep an eye out in case Drake shows nearby."

"All right." I looked on the map, and tried my best to memorize the route. Maybe my compass would help—the bridge was southwest of the Princesse. Trying to sound Ben Green confident, I said, "So where's this painting?"

Agent Stark handed me the rectangular box with a handle. "It's big, but you should be able to carry it. Drake is expecting Benjamin Green, no one else."

I was surprised by the painting's weight. "It's heavy."

"You won't have to go far." Agent Stark handed me a phone. Pretty cool, since my parents never let me have one because it was too expensive. "Henry programmed this phone to receive calls to Benjamin Green's number. When Ben went missing, he had his cell phone on him, but it went dead, so . . . Well, anyway, Drake knows the number, so you should have it on you in case he calls." She slid the phone inside a case that clipped to my belt, and I thought I saw the slightest tremble of her hand. "Don't try to be funny or smart or creative—you get me?"

"No Lincoln Baker, got it. I'm Benjamin Green."

"Don't give them the painting until you have Jacques Mégère. Without him there's no deal for you."

"Got it."

Agent Stark walked me out, and put me into a cab—not Guillaume's. "Before you go: watch out for this girl." She showed me a photo of a skinny girl in faded jeans, with brown hair in a braid down her back.

"That girl looks worried." I actually felt a little sorry for her. "Who is she?"

"This is Françoise Mégère, Jacques's thirteen-year-old daughter. Her mother, an American, died when she was young." Agent Stark sighed. "The reason we recruited Benjamin Green—a kid her age—was so he'd befriend her and she'd tell him the evil *Mona Lisa*'s location. That didn't work."

Thinking of how much I hated the guy, I was happy. "I take it Françoise and Ben didn't become best buds."

Agent Stark pointed at Françoise. "You'll want to keep an eye out for this girl. She's very . . . determined to get her father back. She could mess up the exchange."

"How?"

Agent Stark didn't answer my question. "Just keep an eye out for her." She tucked away the photo, told the cabbie where to go, and wished me luck.

I kept the box on the seat next to me and I glanced around, checking traffic. After being followed by that compact red sedan, I was feeling a little paranoid. But it was a quiet ride. The cabdriver dropped me off on a street corner south of the bridge, and that was it. I was on my own, with this weird box and my skateboard.

This Pont Neuf was really something: white stone, huge

arches, and ornamental carvings. Dad would've loved seeing it. Good thing the painting box banging against the back of my legs reminded me why I was here:

Get Jacques Mégère.

Give Drake the painting.

Go home.

Simple, right? Across the bridge, I could see a giant cathedral with a big dome and ornate towers. I was pretty sure it was Nôtre Dame.

I walked along the Seine. The sightseeing boats in the water were nicely covered in glass to keep the tourists warm and toasty, and I wanted to stop to zip up my jacket, but there, about a hundred yards ahead, was the bridge.

Then there I was on the bridge. I looked around for the bad guy—Drake was supposed to be here, but there were no obvious suspects.

A couple kissing (yuck). An old lady on a bicycle, businessmen in a hurry, talking on the phone. Tourists snapping photos, but no slick-haired dude in a long coat—so no Drake. No Jacques Mégère. And he would be easy to spot with his nutty hair and all.

I sat on a sidewalk bench with the box on my knees, feeling sort of stupid. Freezing my butt off. I got up, started walking on the bridge again to stay warm, all the while keeping an eye on the crowd. Some big French man looked miffed when I bumped him with my painting box, so I apologized.

Where was this Drake guy? I checked my Ben phone, and saw it was five minutes before twelve. I walked back to my side of the bridge, to my frosty bench. Clutching Dad's compass, feeling paranoid. As I sat there, checking the phone again to see only a minute had passed, I had a scary thought.

What if Drake didn't show? I needed this exchange to happen to save my family.

I was lost in thought, so when my phone rang, I jumped. Fumbled, almost dropping the thing. It took me a second to figure out which button to hit, and then I answered.

"Hello?"

Silence.

I waited a second. "Anyone there?"

"Did they give you this number?" An intense voice that sounded vaguely familiar.

"Who is this?"

"Who is *this*? I should be asking you."

I looked around and across the bridge, but a large group of kids on some kind of field trip blocked my line of view. I was in trouble. And I realized that all this time I'd been sitting around, I never hooked up the translator Henry had given me. At least the person on the phone spoke English. "I'm here for the exchange," I said, hoping that was the right answer. "Let's get this over with already." I was trying to sound tough.

"Identify yourself," the guy demanded.

"Benjamin Green."

"Negative."

"Actually, it's positive. Or whatever. I'm Benjamin Green."

"Negative. You are not Agent Green."

"Yes, I am." I could do this all day.

A pause. "I have visual contact."

"What does that mean—you can see me?" I stood up, dropping the box to the ground so I could glance around, behind me, even down to the Seine, in case the person on the phone was on a boat or something.

"I know that is a fake painting," the person on the phone said.

"No, it's not."

"Yes, it is."

"It's not." This was worse than arguing with Mom.

"It is." A sigh. "Look across the bridge."

I did.

And there he was. Benjamin Green stood with his legs shoulder width apart, like he was ready for combat.

I probably looked like I was ready for a shower and a good night's sleep. "You're not missing." I sounded so dumb, but then I was trying to understand. Why was he right there?

"That is correct."

"So why are you across the river?"

"Why am I?"

And then I got it. "Because you're with Drake."

14

TUESDAY, NOON.

I LOOKED AROUND FOR HELP, KNOWING

there wasn't any.

"Who ordered your mission?" Benjamin Green's voice gave me a chill. "Was it Stark?"

I didn't answer.

"The resemblance is good, even if you are in poor shape."

"Thanks."

"I threw my phone in the Seine. Procedure," Ben said. "But it looks like they reassigned my number." He chuckled. "And the case, too."

The guy was ticking me off now. "Where's Jacques Mégère?" I was still hoping to get him somehow so I could go home and everything would be all right. There would be no lawsuit, no expulsion, and I could just go back to my lame field trips with Mrs. Valdez.

Benjamin Green shook his head. "You can report back to headquarters, tell them to stop sabotaging my mission."

"What mission? To join the bad guys?"

"Go home," Benjamin Green said, ignoring my question.

I'd love to, but I wasn't about to tell him. "Says who?"

"The real Agent Green."

I clenched my teeth and grabbed the box, ready to walk across the bridge and force this guy to give me Jacques Mégère. "Why are you even here if you know the painting is fake?"

"I have my orders from Drake." Benjamin Green adjusted his feet.

"What orders? Shoot me on sight or something?"

He was silent.

I felt a cold breeze down my neck.

"Stay away from the Mégère bakery if you know what's good for you," Benjamin Green said. Then he tossed his phone into the Seine and quickly walked off into the crowd.

But I wasn't about to let this smug copy of me get away. I rushed across the bridge, slowed by the tourists who blocked my path. By the time I made it across with my stupid bulky box, Benjamin Green was off in the distance, turning left, disappearing from my line of sight.

I had to catch up with him. So I left the box on the Pont

Neuf and ran, watching him turn right down another street just as I turned the corner. Ben glanced over his shoulder but didn't see me.

Following someone is a lot harder than they make it look on TV, by the way. You have to stay back far enough not to get noticed, but that means it's also really easy to lose the person you're following (this would be the rabbit, remember?). After about twenty minutes, Ben went down a side street, and by the time I could safely catch up, he'd disappeared. I checked every narrow alley, every side street, but no Ben. I'd lost him.

Plus, I was also lost myself.

Agent Stark had given me some colorful euro bills that looked a lot like Monopoly money. On a piece of paper, she'd scribbled her phone number. "Call me," she'd said before I'd left the Princesse Hotel. "Agent Fullerton's in the field and may be hard to reach." But I wasn't about to call her, not to report this failed mission. She would just send me home. Pandora couldn't find the evil *Mona Lisa* without Jacques Mégère. And I needed him to get my family out of trouble.

I took a left turn, and suddenly I saw a dragon painted on one of the windows of a bakery—a nice paint job in fine black brushstrokes. The dragon looked serious and a little sad. The rest of the building was painted a cheerful blue. The awning was red. There were baskets of French bread in the window and a really big pie on some kind of turntable. I'd found the Maison du Mégère—how 'bout that, Benjamin Green? I was about to go inside to spend some of those euro bills, when something hit me from behind.

Thud!

Some sort of stick (a baseball bat?) just missed my head, then hit me at the knees. I fell onto the cobblestoned street.

The Tickstick!

Trying to escape from whoever whacked me, I reached behind me but couldn't grab my backpack. I crawled, too afraid to look over my shoulder. If only I could reach Henry's weapon.

I made it to an alleyway, off to the left of the bakery, when someone kicked me in the side.

A very angry face hung over mine. Dark brown hair, a braid dangling with beads, making me dizzy.

Françoise Mégère.

"You," she said in a tone that told me I was in trouble. I know that tone well. She pushed a boot into my stomach, and before I could move she waved a stick.

Then she clutched it in both hands, kneeled on my chest, and looked at me with a fire in her eyes that could only mean something bad was about to happen.

"Benjamin Green," she said in a very mean, mocking tone, "I'm going to kill you."

And she pushed the stick down on my throat.

15

ONE TIME IN KINDERGARTEN, I PUNCHED
a girl in the shoulder. Her name was Nora Maloney, and she took my apple bites with caramel sauce, which were my favorite (this was before I discovered foods that did not belong on the food pyramid). When I tried to snatch them back from Nora Maloney, she flipped her hair in my face, and I punched her. Not *that* hard, and just in her shoulder, but I got into big, big trouble. It was my first of many more trips to the school principal's office, and Dad made me promise never to hit a girl again.

As my head was being rammed into the Parisian cobblestones, I decided this was one of those times it was all right to break the rules. So I kicked Françoise in the shin—

which shifted her just long enough for me to slide away, out from under her stick of death.

"Hold up, now!" My voice was hoarse. I rubbed my throat, which felt . . . well, like a scary girl had just tried to kill me with a stick. "Don't hurt me!"

She crawled away and stood up, wielding her stick over her head. Now I knew why I needed a backpack full of gadgets: to protect me from this crazy girl. "You lied to me!" She bit her lip. "You took my father."

"I didn't take your father," I said, pulling at my shirt. "I'm trying to get him back for you, okay?"

Françoise looked at my neck, then my face, then my neck again. She lowered her stick and stepped toward me.

"Stop!" I yelled in my most commanding Benjamin Green voice.

"You're trying to get my father back?"

I nodded.

She gave me a mean stare but kept her stick low, so I figured I was sort of safe. Françoise gently pulled at the collar of my shirt. Looked into my eyes. Squinted. "You're not Ben." And she stepped back, giving me the once-over, like she was trying to figure all of it out.

I knew that I was supposed to be Ben and that I was not to let my cover slip. But since my not being Ben made Françoise stop trying to kill me, I told the truth. "I'm not."

Françoise pointed to my neck. "Ben has a scratch on his neck."

"Did you put it there?" I pulled at my collar.

"Hah. You're a funny guy, aren't you?" Françoise's English was perfect, but singsongy, like she was speaking French. I figured it wasn't the time to bring that up, though. "Your eyes are different from his, too," she mumbled.

"How?" I stood up, clutching the strap of my backpack, remembering Henry's Tickstick. She shrugged. Then she tossed her stick aside in the alleyway. "So who are you, then? And why are you here? And where is that Ben?"

I tried to think of where to start, but fatigue and hunger were turning my brain to mush. "Is your bakery open?"

"Not for you." Françoise stood there in the alleyway, like she was trying to make up her mind what to do with me. But then her face seemed to soften a little. "We have leftovers, usually. You tell me your story, and you can eat." She wore a long necklace with a key on it, which she tucked back inside her jacket. Françoise went around me and farther into the alleyway.

I followed her past a Dumpster. Françoise used a key from a key chain clipped to her belt to open a white door with a black *M* written on it. We went inside, walking right into a commercial kitchen with stainless steel cabinets, marble counters, and a bunch of ovens lined up against the wall opposite the door. To my right, there was an open door that led to the bakery. I followed Françoise to the left, into a back room that was obviously the family dining and sitting room. The whole place smelled like fresh bread, making my stomach growl.

"Françoise?" an old woman's voice called from a hallway

to the right of the sitting room.

"*Oui*, Nana," Françoise yelled. She motioned for me to sit at the table, and I did. An old lady walked in, smiling when she saw Françoise. And then she saw me. Her smile faded, and she gritted her teeth. "Benjamin!" She spit the name at me. And she slapped me in the face.

"Hey!" I called, clutching my cheek. "What's up with you ladies in this bakery?" I asked Françoise.

When the old lady looked like she was ready to charge me, Françoise laughed. "Nana, stop! This isn't Benjamin— can't you see?"

The old lady looked confused. Then she leaned closer and boxed my ears.

"Hey, hey." I tried to pull away, but let's face it: this lady was old. I wasn't about to push her.

The old lady frowned and looked into my eyes. She said something in French I couldn't understand.

"That's what I'd like to know," Françoise said as she plumped down at the small dining table. "Who are you, really?"

I hesitated. But then I told them everything: about my chicken farm disaster, the government agents, the expensive lawsuit and Dad working at Meineke, and how I was sent to replace Ben since he'd gone missing. Let's face it: my cover as Benjamin Green was blown anyway. I left out the cool gadgets Henry had given me, but then I figured a guy was entitled to a few secrets. Especially when the ladies at the table had repeatedly tried to hurt me.

I don't think Françoise's grandma understood much of what I was saying, because she still gave me the stink eye. After a while she disappeared down the hall where she'd come from, muttering stuff in French.

"I think your grandma hates me," I said to Françoise once I finished my long story.

"She doesn't like strangers, and she hates Benjamin Green. You look like him, so that's enough for her." Françoise just shrugged. "You want some croissants?" She took me into the kitchen, where there was a basket of flaky pastries that looked awesome.

And they were. "These are the best ever," I said between bites. That got me a tiny smile.

"It's the stuff that fell on the floor."

I stopped chewing.

Françoise grinned. "Gotcha." She punched me in the arm.

"Ow." But I kept eating until the whole basket was empty. "I just got here. All I've had is airplane food," I said as I licked my fingers. "How 'bout that big apple pie in the window?" I was up for some dessert.

"Oh, that's a fake. Decoration, to lure customers," Françoise got me a glass of water, and stood with her arms crossed, watching me drink. After a while, she said, "I'm assuming you still haven't found my father. Since you're here, and he's not."

I said, "And the evil *Mona Lisa* is still missing, too."

Françoise nodded, looking troubled. "So they told you

about the Leonardo da Vinci collection."

"Wait—you have more of these?"

"Not evil ones, but secret." She shook her head. "They didn't tell you. Figures. They didn't tell Benjamin Green either, so why would they tell you?" I could see her thinking, making calculations, trying to decide how much she was willing to share. Trying to decide if she could trust me. "Come on," she said eventually, and motioned for me to follow her into the hallway her grandma had come from. "I'll show you the Vault."

"The Vault?"

16

TUESDAY, 2 P.M.

I FOLLOWED HER DOWN A NARROW

hallway. There were pictures on the walls, family snapshots clustered together, just like we had at home. Françoise's dad, younger, next to some guy who looked a lot like him—same arched nose but a different kind of face. Slicker, meaner.

"Who's that guy?" I asked Françoise.

"My uncle Jules. He lives in America." She paused to look at the picture. "We rarely see him, but he came to visit a few weeks ago. He brought me a Barbie." Obviously this Uncle Jules didn't know who he was dealing with.

We hurried by lots of cute baby and little girl pictures. Françoise, I figured, before someone gave her a stick. Down the hall, to the right, there was a wooden door, and I watched

Françoise open it. Inside were a bunch of shelves, brooms, and cleaning supplies.

Françoise turned to face me. "A month ago, I wouldn't have taken you down here. Never. Do you understand?"

I didn't, but I nodded anyway.

She pulled what looked like an old broom handle, tucked in the corner. There was a soft click, like a door being unlocked, and she pushed against the middle shelf. I watched with my jaw halfway to the floor as the whole back wall opened like a door. A cool draft blew our way from the dark opening behind it.

"You have a bat cave?"

Françoise looked at me, confused.

"It's a lair, like Batman—never mind."

"This isn't some cartoon," Françoise said, irritated. "Follow me."

We walked into a small space blocked by a heavy metal door. Françoise stopped to push the door of shelves behind us, and moved a lever that I figured locked it back in place. Then Françoise used the key on the long chain around her neck to unlock the heavy metal door. It shrieked and moaned when she pulled it open. We walked down these old stone steps, like a stairway you might see in a castle.

"This must be good," I mumbled.

The room beyond the door was about the size of our living room, with a low ceiling lit by dangling bulbs. Françoise turned on the lights. Empty storage racks lined the walls to the left and right of us. At the back of the room were empty wooden bookcases, and in front of them a heavy wooden desk with a lamp and a stack of papers on it.

"This is the Vault," Françoise said, sounding sad.

I lowered my backpack and left it in a corner. I still didn't get the big secrecy. "What is this 'Vault'—your storage space? I don't understand. And you know you're out of everything, for what it's worth."

"I know. This was where my father stored the Leonardo da Vinci collection."

"Da Vinci just gave your family stuff?"

Françoise shrugged, like this was no big deal. "He was a family friend long ago. Da Vinci gave some of his notebooks, sketches, unfinished paintings, and a model of—well, never mind, that's not what you're after." Françoise walked along the empty racks, and came to a sudden stop. "Twenty-two B," she said, with a nod to the empty storage rack. "That's where the evil *Mona Lisa* used to be."

I looked at the spot. There wasn't anything to it really, just another rack, much like the ones Dad used to store stuff at the shop.

"The Vault. I think I get it now. You guys were like guards, keeping this Dangerous Double safe. So where did the rest of the collection go?"

"I'm not sure." Françoise's face hardened. "I had not been down here for weeks. Then last Friday, after Papa left for his deliveries, they showed up."

"Who?"

"Agent Fullerton and Benjamin Green. That kid Ben

pretended to be my friend and tried to get information from me." Françoise made a disgusted face. "So after they left, I came down here to look, and the Vault was empty.

"Then later that afternoon, Papa went missing. So my grandmother called the police. They found his van just a few streets from here in an alley. The doors were open, bread everywhere. No Papa . . ." Françoise's voice trailed off. "I think my father knew that someone was about to steal my family's secret da Vinci collection, so he moved the Vault's artifacts to keep them safe."

This was heavy stuff, to have your father be abducted over a dangerous painting in your basement. And here I thought I had it tough with my chicken farm disaster. Even with a lawsuit pending, my life was pretty easy compared to Françoise's. "So now what?"

"Now I must find my father, of course," she said, sounding irritated. "You only care about your precious painting." Françoise turned away from me and from the empty rack.

"That's not true. I care about my family. And to get things right, I have to find the evil *Mona Lisa*."

Françoise leaned on her father's desk, not seeming to listen.

My mind raced, pumped by the lack of sleep somehow. I tried to think of a way we might find a trail, when I heard a scream, coming from above us.

Françoise shoved me aside and pushed open the metal door. I had to really hoof it to keep up—this girl could run. Up the stairs, past the shelves, out the closet, down the hallway with photos, to the kitchen, where her grandmother was screaming.

Grandma followed up with a bunch of super-angry French.

I hurried into the store. And there he was: Benjamin Green.

17

"LINCOLN BAKER," **BENJAMIN GREEN** said from the other side of the counter—thankfully there weren't any other customers. He looked all serious and a little ticked off. "I thought I ordered you to stay away from the Mégère bakery."

"Exactly." I crossed my arms, and then he crossed his. It was too weird, so I uncrossed mine. "You're not the boss of me." Way to sound mature, Linc. "If I want to come here, I can do that. Besides, you're not exactly a great secret agent, are you? You're a bad guy now."

Benjamin Green clenched his jaw. "You don't know what you're getting yourself into, Baker."

He kept throwing my name around. "How do you know who I am?"

"I saw you on YouTube." He gave me a smug little grin. "Covered in chicken poop."

"I love animals—what can I say?"

Suddenly, he stepped close and grabbed my collar, pulling me across the counter. "You're a clown, Baker, and you're getting in the way of my mission."

"Let go of me!" I tried to pull away, but Benjamin Green should've gotten a certificate of merit for shirt holding. The counter pushed into my stomach.

"Go home, where you belong." He shoved me away. "Leave this one to the professionals."

"Like you? You're a crook!" I reached to grab him by the collar of his spotless black wool coat, but he'd stepped back and was too far for me to reach.

"It's more complicated—too complicated for you to get, Chicken Boy." He pointed his finger at me. "Stay away. This case is mine."

"Says who?" Françoise stood in the doorway to the kitchen, holding her stick in her right hand. "How about *you* stay away, huh? Unless you want to bring me my father."

"I can't do that," Benjamin Green said, sounding sincere, even if we weren't buying it. "Trust me when I tell you—"

"Trust *you*?" Françoise looked ready to spit flames.

And then I saw them, right in front of me—I couldn't believe I hadn't noticed them before. Pies! At least a dozen of them. I grabbed one, silently apologizing for wasting great food, and reached back. Focused on my best pitch.

And I slammed a pie right in Benjamin Green's face.

He just stood there, flabbergasted. Thick white cream dripped onto his black coat.

"Is that what it takes to shut you up?" I said. I picked up another pie and handed a third to Françoise. "I think this one's apple. It's food abuse, really."

Françoise tossed her pie, hitting the superagent square in the chest. "Chocolate," she said, smiling, licking some cream off her fingers.

That was enough for Benjamin Green. He turned and opened the bakery door, ringing the little bell. "You'll need more than pies to save yourself next time, Baker."

Françoise's grandmother snatched the pie from my hands and hit Benjamin in the butt just before he closed the door. "Bull's-eye," she said in her French accent.

And we all laughed.

Then Françoise's grandmother pointed to the mess and wagged her finger at me. "You clean it up." Françoise headed for the kitchen, and I was left mopping the floor. And as much fun as the whole pie throwing was, I started to feel kind of down, to tell you the truth.

So far, I'd managed to ruin my cover as Benjamin Green with Françoise in five seconds, and I still wasn't anywhere near getting Jacques Mégère or the evil *Mona Lisa* back. Meanwhile, my family was dodging the lawyer's phone calls over this crazy, expensive lawsuit.

Then I thought of what Ben said.

It's too complicated for you. What was complicated? And why was he trying to get me to leave? I could think of only one reason.

I was getting somewhere.

If I wanted to stand half a chance of getting my family out of trouble, Dad's shop back on track, and me back in Lompoc Middle School taking lame field trips, I had to keep digging until that evil *Mona Lisa* was found. I had to create my own mission. Prove I could be just like Benjamin Green.

My phone rang and I looked at the number—Agent Stark. Probably checking up on me. I hesitated. If I didn't answer, she'd think I was in trouble.

"Hello, Agent Stark."

"Do you have our package?"

"You mean Jacques Mégère? No." I heard her groan. "Drake never showed. But guess who did?"

"I don't do guesses. Just tell me."

"Benjamin Green."

Silence.

"Seems he's not missing at all," I went on. "He's just joined the Drake operation. And they weren't buying your whole exchange. Maybe he's the one who tipped them off about our painting being a fake."

"So no Mégère."

"No." Now I knew what that meant: the mission was a failure. At least I'd gotten some good croissants out of the deal.

"Where are you?"

"On my way back to the hotel," I lied, and hung up.

Okay, so I stalled, but that would only fly for another half hour or so. Next time I talked to Agent Stark or Fullerton, I knew I had to cough up something better than my bakery pie fight. I needed evidence, a clue, something.

I put the mop away in the broom closet, and went back down to the Vault with Françoise to get my backpack. Meanwhile, my brain was going a gazillion miles an hour.

"We have to be missing something here," I said to Françoise. "Your dad saved all the da Vinci collection and the Dangerous Double by hiding them, right? You don't just move a basement full of stuff without leaving a trail of some kind."

"He could have used the bakery delivery van," Françoise said. "But we have no idea where he took them."

I tried to think like my dad. You'd give him a car with any problem, and he could figure it out. Listen and look for the clues, he'd always say. In this case, there was nothing to listen for, but when I looked around, I saw the big desk. "What's up with all these papers?"

Françoise shrugged. "They're just invoices for the bakery. Papa would come down here to do the books sometimes. I think he liked the quiet."

After meeting Françoise's grandmother, I could imagine you might want to hide out in the Vault. "What else is here?"

Françoise opened one of the side drawers to show paper clips, pens, and a box of raisins—boring stuff, and nothing that could remotely be considered a clue. "Papa used to keep a small ledger of the collection with a picture of a dragon on the front, right here on his desk, but it's gone. He probably took it with him." The big drawer had a small, pocket-size book: *Codes and Ciphers*.

"This is cool." I flipped through the tiny book, looking at numbers, codes, boxes with dots in them.

"This was mine once," Françoise said. "I'm surprised Papa had it. He gave it to me a few years ago. He loves codes and puzzles, just like Leonardo da Vinci did." Thinking of her father, Françoise smiled. "Did you know that da Vinci wrote everything in mirror script?"

I didn't. "Why?"

"Nobody knows. He was left-handed, so some think it was so he wouldn't smudge his ink."

"Da Vinci sounds like an odd guy."

"Yeah. Odd but brilliant, like my father." She took the codebook from me and slid it in the side pocket of her faded jeans. The bottom drawer just had a bunch of empty accounting ledgers in it, and a frustrated Françoise slammed it shut, shaking the desk. "It's hopeless."

"I'm sorry, but I have to go." Agent Stark was probably already waiting with a cab to take me to the airport. I hadn't even unpacked that suitcase or slept in my room. "I wish I could stay and help."

"It's not your problem, really." Françoise's head drooped.

I tossed my pack over my shoulder and followed her out of the Vault, feeling like a loser. I'd come all the way to France just to fail on day one. And I didn't even get to use any of my cool gadgets from Henry.

Upstairs, Grandma was serving customers in the bakery. Françoise gave me a forced smile. "Good luck dealing with your secret agent stuff. I have to go cancel all our deliveries now."

"Why?"

"No Papa, so nobody to drive the van. Deliveries are half our business."

Now I felt even worse, even if none of the Mégère troubles were my fault. I headed for the side door that led to the alleyway. Just over an hour earlier, Françoise Mégère had tried to kill me there with a stick.

Françoise walked over to the far end of the kitchen and pulled a big notebook from a drawer. She flipped it open and frowned. "Weird."

"What?" I stood in the open doorway, feeling the cold November wind that was waiting for me outside.

"The order schedule makes no sense," Françoise said, pointing at the page, then flipping to the next. "Who is this Hendricks customer? And look at these numbers! We're not going to deliver four hundred and twelve loaves of bread to anyone."

I walked over and looked at the order book Françoise had been poring over. I couldn't read any of the scribbles that were in there, except for the number: 412. "What's up with the four hundred and twelve loaves of bread? Is that weird?"

"We can't fulfill that kind of order. And this customer I don't know—Hendricks isn't even a French name."

412. I thought of the little codebook we found in the Vault. And I felt a lightning bolt of excitement. "Maybe . . ."

"What?"

"It's a code!"

18

"IT'S A MESSAGE FROM YOUR FATHER."

Okay, so maybe I was letting my imagination run wild a little, but then why not? We were talking about an evil *Mona Lisa* painting, a Vault with a secret Leonardo da Vinci collection—a hidden code seemed to fit the mood, right?

Françoise frowned and went back to the order book. "This name shows up on more pages. And there's a different number with each one."

"Let's write them down. See if we can get it," I said.

Françoise dug into her pants pocket and tossed me the codebook. Then she ripped a blank page from the order book, took out a pen, and clicked it. "All right, let's get these numbers on paper."

"Go back in the book. See when this name Hendricks first showed up."

After a lot of flipping and scribbling, we had a bunch of numbers that followed the name Hendricks in different orders. Françoise stopped writing and stared at the page. "What does this mean, Papa?" she mumbled. After a while, she shook her head. "I don't know the name."

"Could it be someone your dad works with?"

Françoise shook her head again. "And what are all these numbers?"

I flipped through the book, looking for the code, then I saw one that seemed to fit. "It's a book code. The numbers translate into letters." I scanned the description. "The message is in the letters, and Hendricks tells us where to find them, I think."

"There are three sets of numbers for each delivery, and all of them start with four one two. Each number after that is smaller." Françoise bit her lip. "This is driving me nuts."

"Your mom was American, right?"

Françoise nodded.

"Maybe she left a book behind written by someone named Hendricks?"

Suddenly, Françoise laughed. "There's this chef named Veronica Hendricks. Mom used to love her cooking show, and"—Françoise reached up to the top shelf—"we still have her book!" She pulled out an old hardcover with a brown-haired lady in an apron on the front. Her hair was that weird, flippy style from decades ago. The title was *Cooking in a*

Hurry. "Right here. So now what?" Françoise looked at me.

I stared at the numbers again:

412-1-1

412-1-20

412-6-1

412-7-3

412-7-8

412-7-9

412-1-20

412-1-4

412-1-7

412-8-9

412-9-18

412-1-8

"Move to page four twelve," I said. "Then the second number is the line, and the third is the letter, the codebook says." Page 412 had this recipe:

GRILLED CHEESE AND BACON SANDWICHES

Ingredients for four sandwiches:

8 slices of white or wheat bread

16 slices of cheese

Bacon bits

2 tablespoons of butter

Butter the slices of bread, add cheese and bacon bits, and make a sandwich. Preheat skillet with one tablespoon of butter. Cook 4–5 minutes on each side, until light brown.

Serve with soup on a busy night.

"Sounds tasty," I said.

"Never mind that," said Françoise. "What is the message?"

19

READING THIS RECIPE MADE ME THINK that Dad and I could write a cookbook, too. Grilled cheese sandwiches were a staple meal at the Baker house, especially when Mom was working double shifts.

"G . . . o. Then there's a number two," Françoise mumbled.

"So 'go to' is the first part." I tried to look over her shoulder, but she just brushed me away. "What does it say?"

"Go to . . . the . . . o . . . l . . . d . . . a . . . r . . . c."

"Huh?"

"There's only one old arc I can think of." Françoise slammed the book shut and smiled. "He's telling me to go to the Arc de Triomphe."

* * *

It was pretty obvious that Françoise would've been just fine if I didn't come along: she rushed out of the bakery without a word to her grandmother and hurried across Paris. I was glad I had my skateboard with me. This girl had really fast legs.

But somewhere around the fifth or sixth side street, she just . . . disappeared. I looked back, up and down some other alleyways, but Françoise was simply gone. What the heck? Did she find those flying shoes from the Vault or something? Whatever magic trick she used, since I'd basically just been following her, I had no idea where I was.

I was lost. In Paris, in the middle of the afternoon. And I know it's really uncool to admit this, but I actually missed Mom. She would have a detailed map of Paris in her purse, plus a snack for the road, and we would be on our way to the Arc de Triomphe, no problem. In fact, Mom would never just follow anyone without paying attention.

But there was no time to cry for my mommy—I had to find Françoise, and to do that, I had to get to the arc. I looked around. There was a little café, a store that looked like a pharmacy, and another bakery, but nothing I recognized. I could call Agent Stark and ask her to come get me. She'd give me one of her disapproving huffs, the kind that told me that she knew this was a bad idea. Me, in Paris. Impersonating super junior agent Benjamin Green.

And earlier, I'd told Agent Stark that I was on my way back to the Princesse. If I called her now, she'd just take me to the hotel to go home.

I dug into my pocket for my phone, and I pulled out the business card I forgot I had. And smiled. Because now I had a way to make it to the Arc de Triomphe after all.

Guillaume took up two parking spaces, one of them a handicapped one, and honked his horn. "Lincoln, yes?"

"That's me," I said, a little impressed with myself for finding a better solution than calling Agent Stark and also for going back to being myself. "I need to go to the Arc de Triomphe," I said, buckling my seat belt.

Guillaume laughed. "That's all?" And he kept laughing as he pulled into traffic, narrowly missing at least three cars. "It will take a while, so get comfortable, Lincoln." Just a few minutes, a long, tree-lined lane and a sharp turn later, Guillaume slammed his brakes. "Here we are." He laughed again.

"I was right around the corner?" Boy, did I feel like an idiot now.

"Yes. It's funny, no?"

"No." Actually, it was kind of funny, so I laughed.

"You call me, and you will find your way, even if you are around the corner, okay?" Guillaume leaned back and laughed. I tried to hand him some euro bills, which he declined. "No, no, my friend. This one is for the house."

He meant on the house, but I wasn't about to correct the guy, with him being so cool about this ridiculously short trip and all. I tucked my money away. "Well, thanks."

"No problem." Guillaume looked serious now. "You

remember to call me when you need help."

I could stand to have a friend who didn't try to run away from me all the time, so I agreed and got out.

You know those pictures of famous monuments you see in your history books? The real thing is nothing like them, let me tell you. This arc was at least 150 feet tall, from what I could tell. You could see from a distance that a bunch of stonemasons spent decades making it beautiful. A big traffic circle surrounded the monument. I was across the street, so I figured I'd pull out my skateboard and go find Françoise. Tell her how you're supposed to leave no man behind and all that.

I set my board on the pavement, watching the traffic zoom by. It was crazy—there was almost never a break in traffic. *Almost* never. If you paid attention, you could see there was a flow, with gaps just wide enough for a skateboarding Chicken Boy to make it across. And that big, wide traffic circle was just waiting to be skateboarded, let me tell you.

Concentrating on the traffic pattern, I stepped on my board. The second I was ready to ride, someone yelled "Stop!" and grabbed my backpack. A cop, no doubt about it. This French policeman had a dark-blue uniform and a round face with a very mean expression. "No skateboarding!"

"I'm just trying to get to the arc," I said, pointing across the street. "That's not illegal is it?" Maybe this policeman was one of those skateboard haters.

The cop pulled me back onto the sidewalk. People were gawking at us, but he motioned for them to move along already. "You take the tunnel, young boy," he said to me as he reached to take my skateboard. But I wasn't going to let him—it's a good board, my latest birthday present.

"The tunnel?"

The cop pointed farther around the big circular sidewalk we stood on. "Over there. Tourists take the tunnel underground to get to the arc."

An underground tunnel—that made sense. Traffic wasn't exactly slow over here, and there were no crosswalks or lights. I should have paid attention a little more. "Okay." I clutched my board and started to walk.

"Stop!" The cop pulled my backpack again. "You are still getting a ticket."

"A ticket? No, you can't!" That would mean I'd get into trouble with Agent Stark. And right now, staying off her radar was a top priority. "No, wait. I didn't know I was supposed to use the tunnel."

The policeman pulled a notepad from his jacket and smiled. "Ignorance is bliss, isn't that what you say?"

"No." I was about to try using my charm to stop the policeman from writing a ticket, when I saw Benjamin Green. He stood under the arc, right next to Françoise. She said something to him, looking serious. Why was she even talking to him? I thought she hated the guy and that she was ready to kill him. Then the penny dropped.

She thought he was me.

"No, no. Françoise!" I called but there was no way she could hear over the traffic. What was Green doing and what was he saying to her? What if she gave him the next clue—*our* next clue?

The cop was writing on his pad, looking determined. "Your name?"

I clutched my board and looked across the giant traffic circle at Françoise and Benjamin Green, talking like they were friends. Was she smiling? This was bad, really bad. I wished Françoise had her deadly stick.

"Your name," the cop ordered, raising his voice. "NOW!"

If I was going to get a ticket, I might as well go and skateboard across the street and get my money's worth. Stop Benjamin Green from taking my place.

"Hey!"

I dropped my board onto the pavement and hopped on.

I heard the horns blaring, the cop yelling, the cold Paris wind buzzing against my eardrums.

And I rushed across to the arc, ready to charge Benjamin Green.

20

AS COOL AS IT WAS TO ZIP ACROSS THE street to the Arc de Triomphe while a cop was yelling at me, I don't recommend it as a strategy when you're visiting Paris. As it turns out, my cranky policeman had lots of friends, and by the time I reached the Arc de Triomphe plaza, three of them were ready to take me down.

"No, no," I said, raising one hand, holding my skateboard in the other. "I was just trying to get to a friend, see?" But Françoise and Ben were both gone.

The cops were actually really nice, even if they did arrest me on the spot and make me call Agent Stark. The policemen joked around about me trying to get to a girl, and I didn't want to argue, since it seemed to make them happy.

Agent Stark showed up with Agent Fullerton. Fullerton immediately worked on befriending the cops, giving me a wink, telling me everything would be okay. Stark didn't even try to hide her annoyance with me. She filled out some papers and made an effort to smile at the cops, which she obviously wasn't very good at. After about twenty minutes, they went back to their posts, and I was left with Agent Stark. Fullerton joined us after walking around the monument for reasons I didn't get.

"You said you were on your way to the hotel," Agent Stark said.

"I took the scenic route."

"Of course. You haven't even been in Paris for a day, and you got arrested already." She folded the report in half. "That's a record even for you, isn't it?"

"Hey, I'm not some kind of criminal."

"Give the kid a break, Stark," Fullerton mumbled.

I glanced around, over Agent Stark's shoulder, and around the arc. But still no Françoise or Benjamin Green. "He was here, you know, and again earlier at the bakery."

"Who?" Agent Fullerton asked.

"Benjamin Green, who else?"

Agent Stark started looking around, too. "Right here?"

"This guy has joined the other side, and he's not wasting time. He's after the evil *Mona Lisa*, and—"

"Keep your voice down," Agent Fullerton hissed, but the rest of the tourists at the Arc de Triomphe were happily ignoring us. "Are you sure it was him?"

"Yes."

"You need to go home," Agent Stark said. "This is too dangerous."

"But I'm not done!" I told the agents about the clue we found in the cookbook. "What if we can find the missing painting? Would that rescue the mission and get my family out of lawsuit trouble?"

Agent Fullerton squinted. "Yes, it would." Tourists kept passing by, oblivious to what a dangerous weapon was out there, ready to hypnotize them. "I'll just have to run this by the big man."

"Your boss." I assumed he was talking about the guy in the Hawaiian shirt up in the Penthouse.

"You're lucky that I couldn't get us a plane back to the States until tomorrow," Stark added.

"So what's the difference if I roam around Paris a little?" I gave them both my best smile. "I promise I'll behave."

"Call me or Agent Fullerton every few hours," Stark said. "And if you see Drake, or Benjamin Green, call me immediately."

"Of course." I didn't tell her that Benjamin Green had a way of finding me.

Fullerton nodded toward the other end of the arc. "I think that's Françoise over there. Maybe you can ask her what's going on."

I grabbed my board.

"No more run-ins with the police, please!" Agent Stark called behind me.

"Yeah, yeah," I mumbled. I couldn't help it that the

French had no love for skateboarding, right? I walked up to Françoise, who looked nervous.

"Did you see him?" She leaned closer and scanned the crowd.

"Benjamin Green? Yeah, I did. So you knew it was him and not me?" I scanned the crowd, too, but I was pretty sure my noisy encounter with the French police had scared Benjamin Green away for now.

"Of course I knew," Françoise snapped. "What am I, stupid? But I played along and made him think that I had no idea where the next clue is."

"So you found the next code?"

"Heck no, but I didn't want him to know that."

"So you told him you had no clue, so he wouldn't know you had no clue?" This was confusing and sort of funny, too.

Françoise laughed. I was pretty sure I hadn't seen her laugh out loud until then, so I laughed along. With all this chasing across Paris and dealing with the police, it felt good.

"Now what?" I asked her once we stopped laughing. "I think we sent Benjamin Green on his way, so what do we do next?"

"I don't know." Françoise stared up at the Arc de Triomphe while I strapped my skateboard to my backpack. "According to the clue, there should be something here for us to find."

I looked up, too, and it made me dizzy. "This place is huge." I studied the arc, the carved detail up high. Guys on horses, looking angry, ready to charge with their swords pulled. On the walls below it, names were carved into the stone. Hundreds of dead people—it was actually pretty creepy when you thought about it. "You think your father hid a code here somewhere?"

"I don't know how he would have been able to hide anything here. This monument is more than a hundred years old. It's not like he could carve his code into the stone or write it on it, even." She motioned around at the policemen guarding the arc and the traffic circle around it. "There's always someone watching."

"No kidding." I told her about my ticket for skateboarding, and she laughed. "I guess you're supposed to take the tunnel to get here?" I asked.

"We'll make sure we take it on our way out. But first, we have to find out why my father sent me here. Maybe there's a clue on top of the arc." She bought us both a ticket, and we made our way to these really tight circular stairs. "You have to climb two hundred and eighty-four steps to get to the top."

I thought of calling it quits around step 103, but then Françoise had already bought the tickets, so that would be rude. But 284 steps? "Why no elevator?"

"Oh, there's an elevator, too. But maybe the clue is on the walls."

It wasn't. By the time we made it to the top, I thought I was going to die. I was about to complain when I saw the view: all of Paris, wherever you looked. The Eiffel Tower, Nôtre Dame—all of it. From up here, you could see how all the major roads in Paris connected right where we stood. You've been hanging around me long enough to know that I'm never really speechless, but right there at the top of the Arc de Triomphe, I was.

"They call this point the Étoile—the star," Françoise said next to me. "Napoleon built the arc to celebrate military victories. My father used to take me here all the time."

"Maybe you can see a clue from up here?" I was reaching, but Françoise looked so desperate.

"Can you imagine where?" she asked.

We circled the deck—Françoise even made people move so she could look for clues on the stone floor under their feet. That got her a few puzzled looks from tourists and a dark one from the guard.

"There's nothing," Françoise concluded, her shoulders slumped. "I don't understand. Why would Papa send me here?"

"Maybe there's something we missed downstairs," I said, trying to hide that I was just as discouraged as she was. We made our way down by elevator instead of the stairs, which was a good thing. This chase around Paris was seriously draining my energy.

We looped the monument at least a half dozen more times. My feet hurt, and I was getting hungry, but I wanted to find something, *anything* to get us to the evil *Mona Lisa*.

"There's nothing here," Françoise said after another walk around the Arc de Triomphe. "Let's just go home."

"Maybe we can come back," I said, trying to keep some hope alive for her.

"Maybe. This way out," Françoise said. We walked down these wide stairs into a tunnel that smelled like dirt and faintly of pee.

"So now what?" I asked. My voice echoed off the walls and the low ceiling. The lights flickered.

Françoise sighed and started walking faster. "Now we go home."

I hurried to catch up with her, passing other tourists and some guy in overalls, holding a brush. There was graffiti on the walls that he was ready to clean up. And I stopped, because I saw something I recognized. Something I'd seen in *Codes and Ciphers*, the pocket book from the Mégère Vault.

Dots and lines.

"Françoise!" I called, probably a little louder than I should have. Her name echoed off the walls. Tourists looked my way, slightly irritated.

Françoise rushed back, looking irritated like the tourists, but she dropped that attitude once she saw the wall.

"Did you bring your codebook?"

She handed it to me, all while staring at the concrete. "You think this is from Papa . . . ?"

I flipped through the book. "Right, here!" I showed her the page. "It's Morse code."

Françoise walked along the walls, looking at the black dots and lines that looked like some kind of computer code. She almost bumped into the guy in the overalls who was washing the walls. He was muttering something in French, frowning.

"Let's hurry up and write down what's here."

Françoise pulled out the piece of paper she'd ripped from the delivery book, the paper that had our first clue on it. She turned it over and had me scribble down the code:

```
— —
— — —
— ·
—
— —
· —
· — ·
—
· — ·
·
```

Françoise took the paper, and we both feverishly studied the book's page on Morse code. We were so focused on deciphering the message, I didn't see him come up behind her until it was too late.

This kid in a hooded sweatshirt. For a second I thought it was Benjamin Green, but he was too husky. I swore I recognized this guy. I'd seen him before, but I couldn't remember where or when.

Not that it mattered, because he pushed Françoise. Hard.

Before we could do anything, he snatched the piece of paper. And ran.

21

YOU KNOW ON TV, WHEN THE COP TELLS the bad guy to freeze? I never get why they do that—I mean, the bad dude is obviously going to make a run for it. But as the hooded kid took off in that tunnel, that's exactly what I did.

"Stop!" I yelled, going after the guy. He was almost out of the tunnel by the time I caught up and grabbed his arm.

He swooped around and looked at me. Dark eyes— almost black. He had ruddy, acne-pocked skin, like maybe his parents couldn't afford the creams or something. And a military-type buzz cut under the hoodie, as far as I could tell. He clenched his teeth, pulled his arm away.

And pushed me hard with both hands. Sending me flying, with only my backpack to break my fall.

"Hey!" I called, but he was already making a run for it. I watched him head back to the traffic circle, where a dark sedan with tinted windows pulled up and let him in.

He was gone. Along with our paper with the code on it.

Françoise helped me up. "Are you okay?"

"I'm fine," I said, even if my back felt a little sore. "But this kid just ran off with our next clue."

"At least I deciphered the Morse code." She smiled. "It said 'Montmartre.'"

"What's that?"

"It's not *what*, it's *where*," Françoise said in her usual snappy tone. She pointed to the right, where you could see this bright white cathedral on the hill, practically glowing as the sun was setting. "That's Sacré Coeur basilica. And that hill is Montmartre, where the artists used to live."

"That looks far away. It's pretty late." And I was starving, with me skipping lunch and all. It was nearly five. Didn't this girl need to eat?

Françoise shrugged. "We can take the Metro, but it's not so fast from here. That thief in a hoodie might get there before us."

I dug into my pocket. "I have a way to get there fast, if you don't mind a little bumpy ride."

As it turned out, Guillaume was parked just around the corner from the arc, so he was there in a jiffy.

"Lincoln," he said, winking. "You bring your girl this time?"

"I'm nobody's girl," Françoise snapped at Guillaume as she got in.

"Sorry," Guillaume said to Françoise, but then he tossed me another wink. "Where are we going?"

"Over there," I said, pointing to the hill. "What's it called again?"

"Montmartre," Françoise said.

"Ah, it's beautiful." Guillaume cut across traffic to make a turn. "My cousin has a restaurant up there. Moulin de la Galette."

Françoise leaned forward. "That's where my father makes deliveries for the bakery. The owner, Pierre, is his best friend. He's your cousin?" Françoise asked.

"It's a small world, right? Walt Disney said so." Guillaume laughed. "Maybe you can take our Lincoln there to get a meal, okay?" Guillaume said. "Be sure to check out the menu."

"Sure, yeah." Françoise sat back, which was probably a good thing. Guillaume ran a red light to make a left. It was a miracle we didn't get into an accident, and I was glad Mom wasn't here to see me in the cab.

"So where in Montmartre do we go?" I asked Françoise.

She thought about that awhile. "I'm thinking Papa wants me to go to Sacré Coeur. We used to visit the gardens near the basilica sometimes, after making deliveries."

Guillaume came to an abrupt stop. "Here you are. Take the cable car up," he said, pointing at the hill. "Or the stairs, but it's a long way."

I paid Guillaume, and Françoise got out. I hurried to keep up.

"Say hello to Pierre!" Guillaume called before he sped away.

I followed Françoise to get in line for the cable car—the very long line. People seemed to move extra slow, as if they knew we were in a hurry.

Then I saw Hoodie Guy. He was looking out the big square window at the back of the cable car. He smiled and waved the piece of paper he'd taken from Françoise. "Look," I said.

The cable car was still filling with people, but there was no way we would make this one.

"Let's take the stairs," Françoise said. We started running, taking two, three steps at a time—well, at least Françoise was taking three steps at a time. "Come on, Lincoln!"

"I'm trying, I'm trying!" And I was failing miserably. The stairway was crazy long, hundreds of steps it seemed, with trees and pretty lanterns lining it. I tried to make my legs move as fast as possible, feeling Dad's metal compass bouncing against my back as I did.

I watched the cable car begin its climb down below. Françoise was ahead of me a good dozen steps. And all I could think about was how Benjamin Green wouldn't be this slow. He would be ahead of Françoise already, and he'd probably have some supersmart plan to take down the enemy. Me, I had no idea what I would do once I got to the top of this never-ending stairway.

I had to think like Benjamin Green. What would he do, other than run a lot faster?

I thought of my backpack. The gadgets Henry had given me. I could blow up the cable car with my Tickstick! I looked at the people inside the car that was inching its way up the hill—okay, so maybe that was a bad idea. As much as I wanted Hoodie Guy stopped or even hurt, those other passengers needed to stay safe.

The cable car was now just over halfway up the hill. Françoise was at the top, and I wanted to kiss the ground when I reached her. I felt like my lungs were going to explode.

"Now what?" I asked her, looking around. It was like one of those French paintings: old shops with striped awnings, merchants selling fruits and cheeses, necklaces, and touristy stuff in the marketplace. There was even a plaza with a fountain in the middle, right in front of the cable car stop. Nearby, one of the merchants had set up this little fenced area with—you guessed it—chickens roaming around, probably about two dozen of them.

I laughed at the sight of them—I mean, chickens. Seriously? But then I heard the cable car screeching to a halt. We only had seconds to stop Hoodie Guy.

What would Ben do to stop him? I had no idea.

"Bawk," one of the chickens seemed to say to me. *"Baaawwwkkk. Bawk."*

Let's face it: there wasn't time for me to come up with a great, government-approved plan to stop Hoodie Guy. I had to improvise. Reaching into the front pocket of my backpack,

I pulled out Henry's Tickstick.

Then I stopped. What was it again? Was I supposed to take off the cap?

I looked at the cable car that was now unloading its passengers, with Hoodie Guy trapped in the back, waiting for some family with twins in a stroller to get off.

I inched closer to the market, and to the fountain and the chickens. I opened the little gate, but the hens didn't even move. These were happy French chickens. I actually felt a moment of guilt as I thought of what I was about to do.

I grabbed Françoise's arm. "Walk closer to the guards," I sort of whispered. "When stuff goes down, you tell them it was the guy who stole our clue. Hoodie Guy."

"What stuff is going down?"

"Just do it."

Françoise thought of arguing, but then she saw that Hoodie Guy was off the cable car. And she strolled over to the guard.

I looked at the Tickstick, and then I saw the seal—that was it. I was supposed to twist the cap to break the seal, and then I had a few seconds. But was it five seconds or ten? I really should've paid better attention when Henry told me.

Time to find out.

"Here goes nothing," I mumbled and twisted the cap, hoping I still knew how to aim and throw a good pitch. I only had one Tickstick, one shot. So I'd better get it right. Otherwise, some happy brown chickens might get blown up, and even though my love for chickens was at an all-time low, cruelty to animals was not something I wanted on my record.

I reached back.

Focused. And I tossed the Tickstick, right in the deepest portion of the water in the fountain.

Setting off a muffled boom, followed by a huge spray of water. Disturbing the peaceful happiness of two dozen French chickens.

"*Bawk, baaaawwwk! Bawk!*" They scurried in every direction, feathers flying.

Right into the crowd at the cable car stop.

22

NO CHICKENS WERE HARMED DURING the making of this trouble, other than a few flying feathers. Chicken Boy had worked his magic—creating the chaos to set up Hoodie Guy. It was sort of fun, to tell you the truth.

The chicken farmer waved his fist in the air, yelling French stuff. He must've been a kind farmer (unlike Farmer Johnson), because most of his chickens flew only a few feet away. Meanwhile, Françoise nudged the guard and pointed at Hoodie Guy, who was trying to bolt. Making himself look extraguilty.

This was great! The chicken farmer decided to take action himself, stepping over his stressed-out chickens as he rushed toward Hoodie Guy. The guard had the kid by the arm now, and Françoise slipped away into the crowd.

I waved at Hoodie Guy and smiled. Then I quickly grabbed my backpack and hurried to catch up with Françoise.

"Nice one," she said with a grin.

"Lucky pitch," I said, exhaling. I'd fumbled my way out of trouble, but if there was one thing I knew, it was that when the chaos was your fault, you'd better scram in a hurry. It was only a matter of time before Hoodie Guy convinced them that the American kid had blown the water out of the fountain, and I really didn't want to call Agent Stark to tell her I'd been arrested again. I pulled Françoise's arm. "Let's go, all right?"

"This bomb, that was something your friend Henry gave you?" she asked as we made our way to the back of the crowd.

I nodded.

"I should talk to him sometime," Françoise said. "I have some ideas for gadgets I could use."

A crowd had gathered along the cable car platform, but we walked on, toward Sacré Coeur, passing a few stray chickens along the way. "Well, we lost that kid, at least for a while," Françoise said as we sat on one of the benches near the entrance of the church to take a break.

"I know where I've seen him before," I said, grateful to drop the weight of my heavy backpack for a while. "He bumped into me at the airport."

"Here, in Paris?"

I nodded. "So they knew I was coming to Paris to take Benjamin Green's place. The question is: How?"

Françoise bit her lip. "I'll tell you how. You have someone who's working within your organization. A mole."

"Ben?"

Françoise shook her head. "But it can't be him. He was already gone by the time the government found you, right?"

"Right. So the information about me coming to Paris that day had to come from the inside." From Pandora. I felt really worried now. Who could I trust, really? Agent Stark? She was with me most of the time. It would be easy for her to pass information on to the bad guys, and she was always in a bad mood. Henry I could trust, that I was sure of. Agent Fullerton was the one who'd pushed to get me on the team, so he didn't seem a likely suspect.

"Empty your pockets," Françoise said, pulling at my jacket. "Come on."

"Why?" I asked, but I did anyway. There were some coins—both American and euro change, which looked weird together—and a black matchbook.

"There it is," Françoise said as she took it between her thumb and index finger and opened it. She pulled out a small circular device that looked like a computer chip. She handed it to me.

"It's sticky on the back."

"That's so you can easily leave it anywhere. They've been tracking you. That explains why that kid knew where we were: he was just following your signal."

I was speechless. And I felt a little stupid, to tell you the truth. Why hadn't I noticed this matchbook before?

Benjamin Green would've known—heck, even Henry with his so-so field agent skills would've found this tracker.

I looked around at all the tourists walking up the steps of Sacré Coeur. Then I saw the policeman, wearing bicycling shorts. He was chasing after a chicken. "Hang on," I said to Françoise.

All right, so this part of the story has to stay between you and me, okay? See, ever since I helped catch all those chickens at the Johnson chicken farm, I've become something of a chicken expert. You have to be slow and relax. So I walked over, positioning myself opposite the policeman. He was making little clucking noises. Like the chicken would be stupid enough to go for that.

Careful to move slow and casual like, I looped around, and snatched the bird. I handed it to the cop before it could claw me. No more Chicken Boy disasters for me, thanks.

"Thank you, *merci*," Bicycle Cop said. He carried the chicken over to the farmer, taking just long enough for me to stick the tracker under his saddle.

"Nice one," Françoise said. "I thought you were going to feed the tracker to the chicken."

"That would be animal cruelty. And I love chickens." We watched the cop get on his bike and ride away. "This should keep Drake's guys entertained for a while."

It was dark out now, and I was feeling the day in my legs. But there was no stopping Françoise. That girl was like one of those butt-kicking cartoon heroes—she never stopped. This mission was wearing me out, to tell you the truth, and my Benjamin Green boots weren't all that comfortable.

But we kept moving and headed into Sacré Coeur, which was a giant church. Looking up at the arched windows, carvings, statues, paintings, I was getting dizzy. Stone and echo everywhere, colorful mosaics—now this was a field trip.

"How do we know where to find the next clue?" I whispered, feeling like I was being too loud for a church.

"To the courtyard," Françoise said. "I'm sure Papa wants me to go there." We went outside, to a huge garden with little trees. Mom would love how fancy and tranquil it was all at the same time. Even if it was pretty cold and kind of dreary, the garden was beautiful. I followed Françoise, who was standing near the fountain in the center. "It has to be here," she mumbled. She circled the fountain twice. Finding nothing, she reached into the water to pull out some of the coins that were at the bottom.

"Françoise?" I wasn't sure what to do. She could kick my butt twice over—my first meeting with her in the alleyway had proven that. But I knew that pulling coins from a fountain wasn't just trouble, it had to be bad luck, too.

"But it has to be here," Françoise repeated, mumbling now. "Why isn't it?" She sat on the ground near the fountain, dropping the coins in her lap. She was crying.

"That guy was cleaning the wall in the tunnel, remember? Maybe we're missing part of the code," I said.

But Françoise wasn't listening.

I sat down next to her and tried to imagine what it had to feel like to have your father missing, to have these bad guys on your heels as you're trying to follow clues to get him back. I put my hand on her shoulder, and to my surprise, she didn't move or kick my butt in response.

Trying to think of something to say, I remembered the time after my grandma died. We were all at the house, sitting at the kitchen table, with Grandpa looking like someone had just drained him of all his ninja powers. And Mom, who would always bicker with him, just reached over and held his hand for what seemed like forever. Sometimes, shutting up is the best thing you can do. Especially when you're a Baker.

So we sat there a while, freezing in the November dark. Thinking about the warm California sun, my family, that stupid lawsuit. All I wanted to do was make things right. But finding this evil *Mona Lisa* seemed impossible.

Then all of a sudden, Françoise said, "You know, they say da Vinci used to go to the market to buy caged birds, just so he could set them free."

"Sounds like an expensive hobby."

Françoise laughed, and dropped the coins back into the fountain. "I don't know about you, but I'm hungry." Then she turned on her heels. "Let's eat."

23

TUESDAY, 6 P.M.

OKAY, SO AT THIS POINT, YOU'RE PROBABLY

wondering: What will Linc do now? I definitely was, and so was Agent Fullerton. He called me, demanding to know where I was.

"At this place called Montmartre," I said, trailing behind Françoise.

"Did you find the evil *Mona Lisa* yet?"

We walked down the winding little streets of Montmartre, where streetlights seemed to be popping on as we passed by. "I'm hot on the trail."

"Maybe Agent Stark was right," Agent Fullerton said.

"About what?"

"She says—" Agent Fullerton stopped. Then he snapped,

"You find the next clue, you call me first."

"Sure, yeah," I said, and hung up.

I hurried to catch up with Françoise at the other end of the plaza. Under the streetlights there were artists everywhere, paintings on easels, even an old-fashioned puppet show where little kids were gathered on a small patch of grass despite the cold.

And then my phone rang again—I felt like customer service. This time it was Agent Stark.

"You were supposed to check in with me, remember?"

"Sure, I remember."

"It's been a few hours. Where are you?"

"I'm busy." I told her I was at Montmartre, and about to find the next clue. So maybe I fudged the truth a little.

"You have until noon tomorrow."

"No problem."

"You find anything, call me first," Agent Stark said. "Good luck." For partners, these agents sure didn't talk to each other a whole lot.

I caught up with Françoise. She looked tired and defeated but seemed to brighten when we reached this big windmill, with an attached building in front. When I realized that it was a restaurant, I lit up, too. I was starving.

Inside, it was dark but cozy, and smelled moldy and damp, but also like someone was cooking a stew. I'm pretty sure I drooled a little I was so hungry.

"Françoise?" A short, bald man with a round beer belly came out from behind the bar. As he walked closer, he smiled big. "Françoise!" He kissed her on each cheek, like the French do. But then he held her shoulders, and his face was sad. "My girl," he said, wrapping her in his arms. They stood there for a good minute.

Making me feel really awkward. To make it worse, my stomach was growling, what with all the good food smells. I was dying to taste whatever deliciousness was being cooked.

Eventually, the guy let her go. "Any word on Jacques?"

Françoise shook her head. "I wish."

"How are you and your grandmother holding up? I offered to send over one of my staff to help, but she wasn't having it."

"That's Grandma. And we'll be okay. " Françoise jutted her chin with pride. "Papa will be home soon, I'm sure of it."

Pierre turned his attention to me. "And you are Françoise's friend."

"Lincoln Baker." We shook hands, and he told me he was Pierre, which I had already guessed from what Françoise said during our cab ride to Montmartre. There was a tattoo of a yellow and red flame on his wrist, just like I'd seen on Guillaume. Maybe it was some kind of family thing?

"Are you hungry, Lincoln?"

"Starving."

Pierre laughed, and motioned to a guy behind the counter. He brought out two big bowls of stew with a huge loaf of French bread. We sat at a table in the corner and ate—and I'm telling you this French stew and bread was like the best meal I ever had. While we scarfed down our dinner, Pierre went on to tell me all about his restaurant. How it had been painted by lots of famous painters, like Vincent van Gogh, Renoir, and even Picasso.

"I am glad you made it here," Pierre said. "Last week, Jacques came. He told me the Vault is in trouble."

Françoise froze. "My father talked to you? And you only tell me this now?"

"You needed to eat." The man had a point. Pierre lowered his voice and leaned closer to the table. "The ledger of the collection was stolen, Jacques said."

"Who took it?" I asked.

Pierre shook his head. "If Jacques knew, he didn't tell me. He was worried the Dangerous Double would be next, so he moved it. Jacques left you a message, Françoise." He got up, reached under the bar counter, and came back with a paper menu that he slid across the table.

"This is just a menu," Françoise said. She opened it and shook her head. "I don't get it. We already ate." She tried to slide the menu back across the table, but I snatched it.

There was a picture of the windmill on the back, plus its history. Someone had drawn a border around all this with squiggly boxes and dots, probably for decoration. Or maybe it was a message?

"Why another riddle? Why couldn't he just tell me where the painting is?" Françoise pushed her bowl aside. Is this girl forever angry at everyone or what?

Suddenly Françoise pulled on my sleeve. "Linc! Look outside."

I glanced up, but the light inside the restaurant made it so I was looking at my own reflection in the window.

My reflection moved, but I didn't.

Then it gave me a stern stare down. Benjamin Green–style. He was right outside!

"I'll get you now," I muttered. Tucking the menu in my back pocket, I ran for the street. Outside, the cold wind made my eyes water, and I blinked. Looking for my annoying double—and there he was! Standing right next to the puppet theater, under a streetlight. Like he wanted me to catch him.

But then he took off, disappearing behind a fruit stand. I sprinted after him, looping between the tourists, market stands, and painters. Had I lost Ben, again?

No, there he was! He stopped at a market stand that had leather purses on display. I rushed to catch up with him while he stood there, looking at the vendor.

And he grabbed three purses.

My double ran off. Away from the market, into an alleyway. Without the streetlights, it was so dark, I could barely make out where he was now. But then he jumped out in front of me, seemingly out of nowhere.

"Here you go!" Ben tossed me the purses. Before I could answer, he sprinted into the darkness with that same smooth pace I'd seen in the training videos.

You know when you get that feeling that the rug's been pulled out from under you? I had it, for just a split second as I clutched those stupid purses. Right before someone pulled me back by my left arm.

I turned to face a very stern set of dark eyes. I saw a blue uniform, a policeman's hat.

A cop.

"Is this him?" the policeman asked, glancing over his shoulder at a short, angry-looking skinny guy. The purse vendor.

He snatched his purses from my arms. *"Oui."*

I didn't need to know French to figure out what just happened.

I was busted.

24

AS I SAT IN A VERY CHILLY INTERROGATION
room, I was pretty sure of three things:

I'd been arrested. Again.

Ben had stolen those purses, so for once, it wasn't actually my fault.

This French policeman really hated my guts.

"Sssspeak!" he yelled at me. His hat was off now, and his thinning black hair stood up all over the place. Between that and his bulging eyes, the guy actually looked kind of funny, though I was smart enough to know this was not a good time to laugh.

"Admit it, young boy!" He leaned on the small table between us.

"I have no idea what you're saying," I said for the umpteenth time. "*Oui?* I don't know."

He smiled. And then he left the room, like I had given him what he wanted to hear. This was not good—in fact, this was really, really bad. The policeman left me sitting there for a long time, wondering what had happened to Françoise. Maybe she would come bail me out?

And I thought of my family, the lawsuit, and my chances of succeeding on this mission. Right there in that French interrogation room, I put my odds at roughly zero. Let's face it: Benjamin Green won. Agent Stark, Fullerton—they were right when they said I wasn't good enough to be a junior agent. I couldn't even keep my cover as Benjamin Green.

I was a junior agent failure.

The door opened, just as I was beginning to feel even sorrier for myself. I heard talking in French. Someone laughing—a woman.

Then Agent Stark walked in, still smiling and laughing with the cop. I couldn't believe my eyes: Agent Stark, actually laughing? But when she saw me, her smile faded in a hurry. "All right, let's go."

We took a very quiet taxi ride back to the hotel. I actually missed Guillaume—he would've cheered me up. Agent Stark just sat there with her arms crossed, silent the whole way home. Not that she had to say anything. This was another Linc disaster—no need to point out the obvious.

The cab dropped us off in front of the Princesse. Agent

Stark paid, and turned to look at me. "Perhaps we should have explained at the beginning of your assignment that you're not supposed to get into trouble with the police."

"But I didn't!" I yelled, trying to defend myself. "Well, I did, but it wasn't my fault. It was Ben, he stole those purses and—"

Agent Stark raised her hand. Her face looked even darker than usual. "I don't want to hear about it. Right now, I have to find a way to convince my boss that your Montmartre stunt with the chickens was worth it."

"You heard about that?"

She nodded. "Chickens again. Really?"

I shrugged.

"The boss barely went for your plan to follow those clues that Jacques Mégère left. Now I'll have to write a lengthy report, detailing what happened, accounting for the expenses." She rubbed her neck.

We walked inside, and the receptionist greeted me with a smile. "Back so soon?"

I gave her a confused look—I mean, I'd been gone all day, right? Nothing soon about that. But before I could say anything, Agent Stark pulled me along. She pushed the elevator button. "I'm glad you're having fun with Françoise, but we're running out of time here. Retrieving the evil *Mona Lisa* is our mission—you understand?"

"Yeah." I felt uncomfortable and disappointed in myself. Like I'd let Agent Stark down. The elevator rang its little bell, and we both got off.

"Our plane leaves tomorrow afternoon at two. We have less than a day, or our mission is considered a failure. Try not to get arrested anymore, please?" Agent Stark walked to her own door. "Get some sleep, Linc."

"Ben, you're supposed to say Ben," I mumbled, but she was already gone. Someone had left my backpack by the door. Françoise? It had to be. I looked up and down the hall, wondering if she was still here, but no dice. This was weird.

I checked the time on my Ben phone—ten o'clock. It was nine hours earlier in California, which put the time right around one in the afternoon back home. To feel better, I picked up the phone and dialed.

"Lincoln?" The line crackled.

"Hey, Dad. How are things in Lompoc?"

"They're great. Yeah." That was Dad-speak for not so great.

"Mom told me you had to get a job at Meineke. I'm sorry, Dad. It's all my fault."

"Linc, it's fine. It's just temporary, I'm sure of it." He didn't sound very sure. "And the other guys at the shop are all right. So, how's boot camp?" Way to change the subject, Dad.

"Boot camp, right." I looked around my hotel room in Paris, wishing I could just tell him where I was. "It's great. I'm having fun."

"Fun, at boot camp?"

"Well, I'm learning things, so it's that school kind of fun," I said, trying to recover. Of course boot camp wasn't

145

supposed to be fun. "I'm running a lot, so that's good. Getting in shape and all that. How's everyone at home?"

"Let's see: Grandpa lost his hearing aid. I think he likes it, because he can't hear your mother."

I laughed.

"He's supposed to get an appointment to replace it on Friday. Your mom is trying to get him in sooner."

"How's Mom holding up?"

"You know, working lots. She's setting up some taxi service to get Grandpa to his appointment since I picked up extra hours at the shop. We need some help."

"Sorry, Dad."

"Don't be. Not like you could drive him anyway, champ. Oh, I'm supposed to ask you if you're eating well."

I thought of the Mégère pastries, and the Moulin de la Galette stew. "The food is outstanding, Dad. Tell Mom not to worry."

"I will. How are the other kids there at boot camp?"

That would be Henry, Françoise, and Benjamin Green. "They're okay. There's this one guy who seems determined to get me."

"Just stay out of his way," Dad said. Easier said than done.

"What if I can't?"

Dad was a silent for a good few seconds. "Then you beat him at his own game." That was a very un-Dad-like thing to say, so I wasn't sure what to do with it. "I know life's tough for you there at boot camp," Dad said, "but I have faith in you, Linc. Just . . . don't try to be someone you're not, okay?"

That was exactly what I was doing. Not that I could tell Dad. "Okay."

"All right, I should go," Dad said. "I'm just home on a lunch break. You were lucky to catch me."

"Have a good afternoon at work," I said, feeling a brick inside my stomach. "I miss you guys."

"And we miss you. Hang tough, Linc."

I stared at the phone for a minute after I hung up. Talking to Dad, it felt like I'd been away from home forever. As cool as Paris was, I was ready to crawl back to the Lompoc fog. Looking for the evil *Mona Lisa*, there seemed to be roadblocks everywhere I turned.

Maybe Dad was right. I had to get back at Benjamin Green. Take care of him before he framed me again. The trouble was, I didn't even know where he was. So how could I flush him out?

I stretched out on my bed, staring at the white plaster ceiling. It was all I could think about now: how to beat Benjamin Green. I had to find him and get him busted like he'd done to me.

So how could I find him?

25

PLACE: PRINCESSE HOTEL IN PARIS

TIME: WEDNESDAY, 8:15 A.M.

STATUS: HUNTING FOR BENJAMIN GREEN

I BARELY SLEPT, AND BY THE TIME I GOT
up early Wednesday morning, I still didn't have a clue where
Benjamin Green could be. Did Drake have some kind of
headquarters where all the bad dudes hung out? Where did
Benjamin Green go when he wasn't making my life miserable?
He had to sleep at some point. Or maybe Ben didn't need
sleep like normal kids. Maybe he was a robot.

I had to get inside Ben's head. Think like him. And there

was one person who knew Ben better than anyone else.

My pal Henry.

So I decided to stop by the Princesse Penthouse, hoping I wouldn't run into any of the agents or the boss. I didn't need them to remind me that I was running out of time to complete this mission. Otherwise, it was back home to deal with my expulsion and this lawsuit.

The minute the elevator doors opened, I caught a whiff of burning plastic.

"Hey, Linc!" Henry waved to me from the table, where he was holding a fire extinguisher. "Don't come too close! I have a little malfunction going on."

"I can smell that." I got closer anyway and saw a plastic box the size of a paperback. Inside were scorched wires, foam from the fire extinguisher dripping off them. "Are you building another bomb?"

Henry shook his head and put the fire extinguisher under the table. "It's supposed to be an evil detector."

I laughed, but Henry obviously wasn't kidding. "What for?"

Henry rolled his eyes. "So you can detect the evil *Mona Lisa*, of course. In its dormant state, it has a heat signature of exactly twenty point two degrees Celsius. When the painting is exposed to light, it goes to thirty-two point seven degrees."

"How do you know?"

"It was written in one of Leonardo da Vinci's notebooks."

Henry pointed at a pile of books on the floor behind him.

"You read all those?"

Henry shrugged, like it was no big deal. "Most of them." He took off his glasses and rubbed the lenses on his blue T-shirt. "So how are the other gadgets working out?"

"The Tickstick was great." I told him about my Montmartre fountain explosion.

"Nice." Henry smiled, looking proud. "I'll get you this detector as soon as I can get it to stop overheating."

"Actually, I came here to pick your brain." I told Henry about Benjamin Green, and how he'd gone rogue. How Ben pulled the stunt with the purses.

"That's the Twenty-Five Gee Point Three maneuver!" Henry exclaimed, smiling.

"The what?"

"Didn't you read the *Junior Agent Manual*?" He didn't wait for my answer. "Never mind. The Twenty-Five Gee Point Three teaches you how to lose your enemy by pinning a minor theft on him or her."

"So that's what Ben did—follow a junior agent procedure? I should've known that setup was too creative for the guy."

"The book lays out the move step-by-step, with pictures and everything."

I told Henry I wanted to bust Benjamin Green once and for all. "Where could he be?"

"It's a big city." Henry bit his lip. "Agent Green lives for the job. He's a secret agent every minute of the day. It sounds like he's using his training to beat you, so that's your best bet to catch him: think like an agent."

"I was hoping maybe you had a Find-Ben device."

"Sorry. Unless you put a tracker on him." Henry frowned. "Are you sure he joined the bad guys?"

"Positive."

"Then I don't know. The Benjamin Green I know would never go to the dark side."

Okay, so this visit with Henry wasn't all that helpful. It was nine o'clock by the time I left the hotel, and I was beginning to hear the seconds tick by inside my head. Pandora had practically given up on me, but I wasn't ready to just yet. You've been hanging around me long enough to know that I'm sort of stubborn that way.

I had to find Ben. Then hopefully I could actually get to the evil *Mona Lisa*.

I decided to go with Henry's advice: Benjamin Green would think like a secret agent. So I had to think like one, too. On my way out, I grabbed a free tourist map in the hotel lobby. I planted myself on a bench near a park and began to study it.

If I were Ben, where would I be?

I thought of our training and those classroom videos I'd only paid half attention to. I remembered one part: always find an exit, and always keep an eye on your enemy.

Keep an eye on your enemy. I was Benjamin Green's enemy.

Okay, so it was a little weird to think of myself as the

bad guy. But to Ben, I was, right? I'd taken his place for the exchange. Now, Françoise and I were following the clues to get to the evil *Mona Lisa*. I'd stopped his buddy the Hoodie Guy, and ditched the tracking device. Ben had to hate my guts at this point.

So if he was keeping an eye on me, where would he be? Somewhere near my hotel, I figured. I did a terrible job at folding my map, and then I went back to the Princesse, glancing over my shoulder to make sure I wasn't someone's rabbit.

I stood in front of the hotel, and looked around—*really* looked, like a secret agent would. There was a major road just off to my right, so there was your quick exit strategy. Straight ahead, an alleyway, some restaurants, and another bakery. The French were very serious about their baked goods.

But I realized: there wasn't any other hotel nearby. And I felt a chill go down my spine, like someone dropped an ice cube right where I carried my backpack.

Benjamin Green was staying at the Princesse.

It would be the best way to keep an eye on me. And who would know the difference—if he ran into anyone at the hotel, they'd just think he was me. Benjamin Green was doubling as Linc Baker. I laughed—you have to admit that was pretty smart, right?

And I felt really, really stupid as I stood in front of my hotel. I should have known: the strange looks from the hotel receptionist, how she already knew me as Ben when we checked in—*it was because he was already there*. The receptionist saw me *and* Ben. Ben was still staying at the Princesse. He was keeping an eye on me.

So now I had to be smarter than Benjamin Green. I had to flush him out, so he wouldn't be able to set me up again.

Like Dad said: I had to beat Benjamin at his own game.

I walked into the lobby, straightened my shoulders, and walked up to the lobby desk. "Hi, I'm Benjamin Green."

The lady behind the desk smiled. "Of course, Mr. Green. How can I help you?"

I crossed my arms, just like Ben would. Frowned, all serious like. "I would like to check out of my room, please."

26

WEDNESDAY, 10:45 A.M.

FOR MY PLAN TO WORK, I NEEDED HELP.

So I knocked on Agent Stark's door, explained that I had
found their rogue agent Benjamin Green, and that he would
be in the lobby, looking ticked off. I figured he'd gone out,
looking for the next code somewhere around Montmartre,
and he would be back right around then.

I was right. Agent Stark caught Benjamin Green in the
lobby, arguing with the receptionist. And I swear he gave me
a little smile of recognition, right before she escorted him to
the Penthouse in handcuffs.

I was on my way up on the hotel elevator, feeling pretty
smug, thinking about getting some naptime in. But when the

doors opened on my floor, I was blocked from exiting. By the big guy, wearing a green Hawaiian shirt this time. The boss.

"Lincoln Baker," he said as he got on the elevator. "I'm Albert Black. You're with me." Then he laughed as the elevator doors closed in front of us. He had one of those laughs that sounded a lot like a heavy truck rumbling down a street. "Nice, that whole checking-Ben-out-of-the-hotel shenanigans. Couldn't have played it better myself, kid."

"Thanks, I think."

Albert Black used his key and punched the Penthouse button, and then he crossed his arms for the ride up. "How are you liking Paris?"

"It's nice. The croissants are the best." I waited for us both to get off the elevator, and waved to Henry. He had his sleeves pushed up and was working on the plastic box at the big table in the center of the room. He gave me the thumbs-up, which I assumed meant he wasn't setting stuff on fire anymore.

"This way," Albert Black said. I followed him to a room down a narrow hallway, past a closed door, and to a closet-sized room in the back. "Sit." He motioned to one of the chairs and closed the door. He sat across from me. On the table was a red folder, but he didn't open it.

"Is this the part where you tell me about all the stuff I figured out already?"

That surprised him. He looked up at me with an amused smile. "And what exactly do you think you know, kid?"

"Let's see. We can start with the Vault, and how there's a

lot more missing than just an evil *Mona Lisa*." I was ticked off. Pandora had treated me like a dumb kid, and I'd had enough of it.

Albert Black was silent.

"You should have told me the truth," I said.

"Look, you made it this far. We've got Benjamin Green—couldn't have done it without you, so bravo." He gave me a little applause. "Now it's time to go home."

"How about Jacques Mégère and the evil *Mona Lisa*? I've been running all over Paris with Françoise, trying to solve these ciphers that Jacques Mégère left."

"And now it's time to let go." Albert Black pushed the red folder aside. "Pressure's coming from up top to wrap up this expedition. It's costing a fortune, and America is broke."

"So what does Ben have to say about all this?"

"He isn't talking." Albert Black crossed his arms. "The kid's a real tough nut."

"Let me try," I said. I wanted to see Ben face-to-face and hear what he had to say, even if it was nothing. "Then I'll go home."

"You'll go home when I tell you. You're not the one calling the shots around here." Albert Black looked angry.

"Maybe he'll talk to me. Double to double and all that."

Albert Black squinted, like he was thinking about it, but I knew I had him. "Five minutes." He got up. "That's it. Follow me."

I followed the loud Hawaiian shirt down the hall to a locked door. Albert Black unlocked it. "Five minutes," he said with a death-ray stare that made Mrs. Valdez look like an amateur.

I went inside the room and heard the door lock behind me. In front of me was a large, shiny table with just two chairs. One of them had Benjamin Green sitting in it.

He gave me a little nod and narrowed his eyes, which for some reason really ticked me off.

I sat across from him. The table was ginormous and the chair low, which made me feel like a little dwarf. I tried to adjust the chair, but that only made me sit lower.

Ben looked away with a smirk.

"You think that's funny?" It was sort of funny, I knew that, but I just was too angry to admit it right then. "You know, I don't get you at all," I said, with the table up to my chest because my chair was so short. "Benjamin Green, the poster boy junior agent. You're good at everything. Do you know you're in a video they play at junior agent training camp?"

Benjamin didn't respond. He wouldn't look me in the eye.

"What I don't get is why you did this. Why you joined the bad guys—what, for the money?"

Still no response. His face was hard, like a brick wall. He'd obviously decided he wasn't going to talk.

"You know, they were all wrong about you in that video," I said. I wanted to punch the guy. But I decided it was better just to walk away, because in the end, he was the one handcuffed to a chair.

"So what did this mysterious bad guy tell you? Did he promise you millions or something?" I tried to lean closer over the giant conference table, but my low chair made it impossible. And I was angry, so I stood up. "Was that worth selling out your government, the Mégère family, Françoise? Abducting Jacques Mégère?" I leaned on the table. "Do you really have nothing to say?"

He blinked—just once, but it was enough for me to know that I'd gotten to him. I'd been trying so hard to be Benjamin Green, only to feel like an utter loser. But I never stopped to think that maybe I had some skills he didn't have. Maybe not knowing the rules of the junior agent handbook was actually a good thing.

I looked at Ben closely, struck again by how we were mirror images, even if we were completely different on the inside.

And I had an idea.

So I told Ben, smiling. "You know, you setting me up in Montmartre by stealing those purses just gave me an idea."

He still didn't say anything, but his puzzled expression was all the response I needed.

"What was it: maneuver twenty-something of your junior agent rule book?"

"That's twenty-five gee point three," Ben said.

"Whatever. My point is, you lack the imagination to get this whole double thing right. All you do is follow your *Junior Agent Manual*." I had a brilliant plan—a fantastic, scary, fueled-by-anger plan I would have to sell to Albert

Black. I slapped the table. "Thanks, Ben. You've been very helpful." I smiled and turned away. I knocked on the door, since someone would have to let me out.

"Don't you get that I've been trying to protect you?" Ben said behind me. "You don't have what it takes to be a junior agent."

"Oh really?" I said as Agent Stark unlocked the door. "Just watch me."

I walked past Agent Stark, out of the airless room, and down the hall until I found Albert Black. "I'm not going home," I said to him, my hands in fists at my side.

"That so, kid?" He gave me a mocking expression.

"I want to go join them," I said, feeling all superagenty. "I want to take Benjamin Green's place with the bad guys."

27

WEDNESDAY, 11:30 A.M.

HAVE YOU EVER SAID SOMETHING, THEN wished right away you could just take it all back? I did, standing there in front of Albert Black. I really didn't want to join the bad guys. That was a bad, dangerous plan—what was I thinking? But I couldn't exactly stuff the words back into my mouth, so I just nodded. Trying to look really sure of myself.

"All right." Albert Black didn't even hesitate. "Good plan." He grinned. "Wish I'd thought of it."

"Okay." I wasn't expecting that. I figured he'd be putting up a fight, with me being twelve and not exactly super-agent material and all.

"You go to Ben's room, wait for Drake's dirtbags to call

you," Albert Black said. "Then they lead you to Mégère, and we get him. Easy as pie. Be done by tomorrow."

"We're talking about the same guys who trailed me across Paris, who are after a billion-dollar painting no one else knows exists. Easy as pie?" I swallowed. My anger and adrenaline were wearing off now, and I realized how dangerous it would really be to take Benjamin Green's spot in the bad guy's lair.

"Okay, so maybe it's not as easy as pie. Maybe more like as easy as fruitcake." He laughed at his own joke. "Look, kid, you finish the job, and we'll take care of the mess you made back in California."

I wanted that more than anything: to make things right for my family. And I also wanted to finish this mission here in Paris: get the evil *Mona Lisa* and bring Françoise's dad back home. And I wanted to show everyone that Lincoln Baker wasn't a screwup who didn't finish anything he started.

"You'll be done by tonight, I'm sure of it. I'll move the flight to tomorrow."

"Okay." I sensed an opportunity here. They needed me to complete this mission—it wasn't like they had Benjamin Green lookalikes lying around. And it was my idea to take his place. "But I want something else."

Albert Black got up, shaking his head. "You got your deal, kid. There's no more negotiating."

"This is way more dangerous than our original deal for that exchange, and you know it." I got up myself. "I need to know that my dad's business is going to be okay."

"What do you want from me—money?" Albert Black pushed the elevator button and gave me a hard stare. "I don't have any extra. And neither does the government."

"I want broken cars. Business for my father's shop, that's all. He's good at what he does, and he won't rip you off."

Albert Black sighed. "Broken government cars? I'll see what I can hustle up. But you better get your game face on. Time to get to work."

"We have a deal?"

"You have a deal, *Benjamin Green*." The elevator dinged, and I got on. Just as the doors closed, Albert Black's satisfied expression made me wonder if taking Ben's place was really my idea, or if Albert Black just made me think it was.

As it turned out, Benjamin Green's room was on the first floor—which in Europe apparently is like our second floor. After I went to my room to grab my backpack, I found that the hotel staff had put all Ben's stuff back into his room after Agent Stark explained that it was just a mix-up. So I was now officially taking the guy's place. He had a small black messenger bag with a cell phone, notepad, map of Paris, and a piece of rope—to tie me up? Who knew?

Since there was nothing to do but wait, I did what any self-respecting troublemaker would do if he was in someone else's hotel room at lunchtime: I ordered room service. Lots of it: pastries and cake, ice cream and pizza—whatever looked good on the menu. And as I waited, I ate until I couldn't eat any more.

I figured that while I was sitting on this fluffy bed, I might as well get a nap in. This nine-hour time difference between home and Paris was kicking my butt. I was just dozing off when there was a loud knock. But whoever was there didn't wait for me to open the door. They had their own key.

"Benjamin?" an American voice called in the darkness of my room. I recognized it, or at least I thought I did.

It was Agent Fullerton. And he thought I was Benjamin Green.

But wait—why was he here?

Agent Fullerton was a bad guy. That explained why he'd sort of fallen off the radar, and why Agent Stark seemed so ticked off all the time. Her partner had gone rogue, right along with Ben. And he was the mole, the one who'd been feeding Drake information.

"Time to go, Ben." Agent Fullerton gave me a dark look. This was not good.

"Sure, yeah." I blinked. But before I could say anything else, this really big guy came up from behind Agent Fullerton and grabbed me by the arm. "Hey, hey!"

"Quiet!" He dragged me out of the room. Agent Fullerton followed.

I only had a second to snatch my backpack. *My* backpack. Linc Baker's, not Ben's. Because I knew that mine had the tools I needed to get me away from these guys. "What's this about?"

"Don't play stupid," the big guy said with a heavy French accent, as he practically dragged me to the elevator. He had a knife or some kind of weapon that poked me in the back. "You know what this is about, *Benny boy*."

"Actually, I don't. I—"

"Quiet!" We walked past the receptionist, but all she did was smile. Once we were outside, French Guy said, "The boss is going to kill you."

Before I could argue, there was a sharp pain at the back of my head, then nothing but blackness.

28

WHEN I OPENED MY EYES, IT WAS PITCH-
black and I had a splitting headache. There was a rocking
motion, a humming noise, and the smell of gasoline.

I was in the trunk of a car.

Being a Baker, from a family that loves cars, you'd think
I would be okay. But I was scared. To death. I'd seen enough
bad guy movies to know that when they had you in the trunk,
it was not a good thing.

The lid was really close to my head, and there was no
room to move my legs or stretch my back.

I heard laughter from the front. The guy who'd grabbed
me and Fullerton were probably talking about how they were
going to kill me or something. Good times, driving around,

plotting the murder of that pesky Benjamin Green. Only I wasn't Ben.

I moved my fingers to feel for a trunk release—many newer cars had those now, I knew that from Dad's shop—but no luck. Although I did feel something else. Rough canvas, like the fabric of a tent. Or maybe a bag.

My backpack!

The bad guys had tossed my pack in the trunk with me. I smiled there in the dark, but then I realized that I didn't have much to help me in there. I could deploy the chute. But then it wasn't like I could exactly fly away or anything. I planned to hit them with my skateboard when they opened the trunk.

"The boss will be happy. You think he will cut up the kid?" This was Fullerton talking.

"Probably. Drake likes it that way, less to trace," French Guy answered. "It would be a nasty mess, though. This is a rental, man."

I felt a chill. They were talking about killing me, or their boss killing me, anyway. I had to focus on breathing so I wouldn't panic.

"I keep these heavy-duty plastic tarps in the backseat now. See? They cost you a few Euros, but they're well worth it."

I tried to focus on listening, despite the raging panic that made my ears buzz.

"If you're smart about how you lay the tarp, and fold the edges up, tape the corners with some duct tape, it acts like a tray. Keeps the fluids contained."

"I'll have to try that. Thanks for the tip. Last time, it took me hours to scrub all the blood out."

"Uh-huh. I know what you mean."

"How about the big dragon?"

"Not yet. Too valuable."

Dragons? What was this, some wizard movie? Maybe that blow to the head had scrambled my brains a little more than I bargained for.

"And the little dragon?"

Nope, they really were talking about dragons.

"That one will be done soon."

There was a really sharp left turn. I banged against the side of the trunk. Then a right turn, pushing me against my pack.

I reached inside my backpack, but all I had was a translator I didn't need, the tracking device, and the stickers. Just great: I could track the bad guys—but wait! I knew where they were already. Angry and scared, I peeled the back off one of the stickers anyway and pushed it against the side of the trunk. It couldn't hurt. Maybe they would find my body, I thought with a chill. Wrapped inside a heavy-duty tarp, so my blood wouldn't mess up the upholstery.

Then I flew against the back of the trunk as the bad guys hit the brakes. The engine died.

Doors slammed.

More laughter. Panic, inside my chest as I held my skateboard, ready to smack them—bam, bam!—in the head. I'd be quick. And I would skateboard away. I knew how to do that.

Footsteps. A key, turning in the lock. I felt the edges of the skateboard cut into my skin as I clutched it as tight as I could.

Bright light. Laughter. I reached up, but before I could bang anything, I got hit in the head.

And it was pitch-black again.

29

"NICE WORK, GENTLEMEN. NOW, THERE
won't be any unpleasant dealings with the French police,
correct?" That was a new, nasal voice. An American.

"No problem, sir." This was Agent Fullerton talking.
"Nobody saw us. The kid was by himself. Albert Black runs
his operations loose and sloppy." He laughed. "We searched
his backpack and took his translator and tracking device."

They left me my two stickers—useless without the device.

"Good," the other voice said.

I opened my eyes, just a slit. I was on a cold tile floor,
watching several sets of feet. Two pairs of black lace-up
boots—Agent Fullerton plus French Bad Guy, who'd been
talking in the car about the heavy-duty plastic tarps for easy

169

cleanup—and a pair of loafers with tiny tassels. That had to be the boss.

"Very well, gentlemen. You can wait outside while I have a little talk with Benjamin Green here." I closed my eyes. "Should only be a minute, and then you can do what you do best."

There was laughter, followed by heavy footsteps and a closing door.

The rustle of fabric and a sigh near my ear. "You can stop pretending now, Green. I know you've been listening."

I opened my eyes and looked at a bright white smile. Slicked-back brown hair, blue eyes, a face I recognized from somewhere but couldn't place. "Hi," I said, still a little woozy from being repeatedly whacked in the head. I blinked and realized: this was Françoise's uncle, the guy I'd seen in the photo next to her dad, in the hall at the bakery. Uncles Jules.

Our bad guy Drake was Françoise's uncle.

"Get up." Drake stood up himself and stepped back.

I got to my feet slowly, touching my head. It felt wet, and I moved my hand to find blood on my fingertips. I wiped them on my pants, trying not to freak out. When the room around me stopped spinning, I saw it was a big room, with fancy furniture, marble columns, and high windows all around. In a corner, a desk with a laptop computer sat next to a giant whiteboard. It had our two decoded ciphers on it and space for a third.

"Sit down," Drake said as he settled on the sofa. I reminded myself that he thought I was Benjamin Green, who had done something so bad he was going to cut me into pieces.

So I sat.

There was an old, leather-bound book on the table in front of us. It had a dragon embossed and painted on the cover. The Vault ledger! Drake was the one who'd stolen it. Next to the ledger sat a tray of diced fruit and pastries. Drake leaned forward, took a piece of pineapple, chewed it, all while staring at me. "I hate these pastries, don't you?"

"Yes," I lied.

"It seems this city is obsessed with its baked goods."

"All those carbs, yuck."

He laughed. "Exactly."

What were we talking about here?

"Let's cut the nonsense, shall we?" Drake shifted position, and crossed his legs. "You were supposed to be following the girl to Montmartre." That had to be Françoise. "But instead, I hear you're just sleeping in, watching movies—is that it?"

"No, of course not. Sir." People like it when you call them sir, especially when you're apologizing. I figured that out long ago. Right now, I would have to apologize like my life depended on it. Because my life really did depend on it.

"I was gathering intel on this boy we've been seeing her with," I continued in my best Ben voice. "Lincoln Baker, my lookalike." I gave him the Benjamin Green trademarked serious frown. "He's really just a nuisance, but the boy seems to have stumbled onto some useful information."

Drake reached forward to take another piece of pineapple.

171

He raised one eyebrow and said, "This nuisance managed to befriend Françoise Mégère almost instantly, something you weren't able to do even with all your training. Now they're running all over town, deciphering my brother's ridiculous clues." He leaned forward. "And you're useless."

For once, it was Benjamin Green who'd messed up, and here I was taking the blame! I had to think of something, or I would be killed soon. I looked around the room, then at the whiteboard with codes.

Drake brushed some nonexistent lint off his suit. "I don't have room for error in my organization. Your time is up, Mr. Green." And as if on cue, the door opened, and Agent Fullerton and French Bad Guy came in for me.

"Wait," I said, jumping up. "I have the next coded message!"

Drake stopped in his tracks, looking at me. "You found the Montmartre cipher? Where?"

My mind was going a hundred miles an hour. "The cipher . . ." And I felt a dread turn into a brick inside my stomach. Not because I was about to be cut into little pieces, but because I actually knew where I'd seen the next cipher. And I was about to give it to Drake, the bad guy. Not to Françoise.

I reached in my back pocket, where I'd tucked the folded-up menu the day before.

"Le Moulin de la Galette." Drake rolled his eyes. "Of course, that dump." Then he looked back at me. "So the code—where is it?"

I took a breath, and hoped she would forgive me. And Pierre, too. "The menu," I said. "The code is on the back."

I was dead. Dead Linc walking. And not because of these Drake guys, Agent Fullerton, or their heavy-duty plastic tarp system—they needed me now, and I was pretty sure I'd redeemed myself by giving up the menu. It was Françoise I worried about. Once she found out I'd given the enemy the cipher we'd been running all over Montmartre for, she would get the biggest stick in Paris and finish what she started when we'd met.

"You're right," Drake said with a giant white grin on his face. He pointed at the menu, at the pattern of boxes and dots that ran along the desserts. "This is a pigpen cipher." He wagged his finger at me. "You just became my number one guy, Benjamin Green."

Lucky me. "I told you I found it."

Drake handed me the menu, and waved his hand toward the whiteboard, like I was the maid or something. "Go. Write it on the board, find out what it says."

I got up, still feeling dizzy from all those blows to the head. Then I scribbled the boxes and dots on the whiteboard:

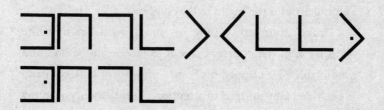

30

SO NOW WHAT? I MISSED FRANÇOISE—
together, we would have decoded this in a jiffy. Especially
since she was the one with the codebook.

"Use the computer!" Drake hollered from his spot on the
sofa while he ate another piece of pineapple. "Find out how
that cipher works!"

I did, despite my pounding headache. But the message
made no sense at all: *home sweet home*. Over and over,
looping around the menu in that pigpen cipher. Huh?

Drake stood up, wiping his hand on a bright white
cloth napkin. "Of course. Leave it to Jacques to be dull and
predictable." He clapped his hands, and Agent Fullerton and
French Bad Guy jumped to attention. "Gentlemen, go get my

brother. My buyer is expecting the painting at one tomorrow afternoon. It's time to finish this ridiculous treasure hunt."

Agent Fullerton nodded, and they left.

"You have Jacques Mégère?" I asked before I could think.

"Of course I do. But you know this, Benjamin." Drake walked over and studied my face. I swallowed, expecting him to clock me because he figured out that I wasn't Benjamin Green. Drake raised his hand, but then gently tapped my cheek. "Those blows to the head really have you all confused. I'm sorry about that. But now we can forge ahead, and collect the millions. Let's go."

"Right." The guy was a weasel. "Where are we going exactly?" I asked as I trailed behind.

"Where it all began, naturally. I should have known it would end up like this." Drake gave me a smile that could only be called evil. "Home sweet home. We're going to Maison du Mégère."

We took a dizzying ride in a shiny silver Mercedes—dizzying mostly because of my scrambled brain. It was dusk, and it took us awhile to make it through Paris rush hour traffic. Drake was a very calm driver, signaling at every turn, coming to a complete stop at every red light. He might be a ruthless killer who took his own brother hostage to make a buck, but he was an A-plus driver.

"How's the head, Lincoln?"

"It's good, I think. It only hurts when—" *He called me Lincoln.*

Drake smiled as he coasted to a stop at a red light. "It pains me to do this, really." Then he raised his hand with a gun in it. Flipped it over, so the butt faced me.

And he whacked me in the head.

I walked in a green field, covered in fog, just like at home. There were brown and white chickens, peacefully doing their pecking thing, and Grandpa in a ninja suit, practicing his moves. He waved as I walked by.

As you've probably figured out by now, I was having some weird blackout. Being hit in the head does that.

Drake smacked me on the cheek.

"Wake up."

I opened my eyes to see that he'd parked right in front of the bakery. It was pitch-dark inside. The car clock told me it was just after six. "Why are we here?" I tried to reach for the door, but realized my hands were bound by one of those plastic snap ties.

"Because of the cipher, of course." Drake sighed. "I hate this place. The smell of the rising dough, the buttery croissants." He opened his door. "Don't try anything. Or I'll kill the girl."

I got out, too, and watched as he took off his suit jacket at the front door, wrapped it around his fist, and smashed the glass with the painted dragon on it. Drake opened the door, then pulled me inside by my sleeve. "Move it."

There was no alarm, no flashing lights. Just the lingering smell of pastries, even though the shelves were empty. It looked sad and a little creepy like this.

"Who is there?" Françoise's grandma called. Every muscle in my body tensed up. If this creep Drake would hurt her—his own mother—I might just have to take him out, even if he did have a gun.

"It's me, Mom. Your favorite son." Jules Drake smiled as he walked into the bakery kitchen and spread his arms like he was ready to hug his mother.

"Jules?" Grandma held a stick, which looked suspiciously like the one Françoise had almost killed me with when we first met. "Is that you, Jules?" Then she looked past us and saw the broken glass.

Quietly, Françoise came up behind her. She was in her same faded jeans, with a big black sweatshirt that looked like it belonged to someone much larger. No stick, just her temper to arm her. "You," she said to her uncle. "I should have known you were the one. Papa always said—"

"Your father is a fool. Hiding away this valuable Leonardo da Vinci collection, our family's property, like only he owns it," Drake said, spitting the words. "And now he has you running all over Paris—his own daughter—to find this evil *Mona Lisa*. Why?"

Françoise spat back, "He's keeping it safe from criminals like you."

"Says who?" Drake picked up the delivery book from the counter and threw it across the bakery. Grandma flinched. "It's time we stopped living like paupers. Time we cashed in on our family's investments. I have a buyer ready to hand over a fortune for the power of the Dangerous Double. Nevermind what the da Vinci collection could bring in."

"But why are you here? The Vault is empty." Françoise motioned to the door that led to the Vault. "Papa knew that once you came back, the Dangerous Double wouldn't be safe."

"The cipher," Drake said. "It said 'home sweet home,' which has to be here."

Françoise laughed. "Your cipher is wrong—there's nothing here. Where did you find it anyway?"

"It was on the Moulin de la Galette menu," I said, watching her smile fade.

"And you figured you'd help my uncle find it?"

"It's more complicated than that, I was told to go, and—"

Françoise crossed her arms. "You were *told*, right. Your mission to find the evil *Mona Lisa*. I forgot. Who cares what happens to my family?"

Meanwhile, Agent Fullerton and his sidekick had shown up, and they started to toss stuff around. Cake pans fell to the floor with a clang, followed by cookbooks, papers, and bread baskets. They used a stool from behind the counter to smash the other windows.

"There's nothing to find!" Françoise yelled at Drake, shielding her grandma, who looked terrified. "Do you really think Papa would leave anything here, knowing you could find it?"

Drake stopped in the hallway, where the dozens of family photos were on display. He grabbed one and pushed it into

Françoise's face. "Where is this?"

She took it and shrugged. It was difficult for me to see, but it looked like a family get-together—dinner in front of a small house with lots of trees all around. Françoise hesitated.

Drake snatched the frame, then pushed it until it was just an inch from Françoise's face. "WHERE?!?"

She stepped back and whispered something to her grandma. Then Françoise turned to her uncle. "You let Grandma go, and I'll tell you."

Drake waved his mother off.

"Go," Françoise said softly.

Grandma waved her stick at Drake, tears streaming down her face, then disappeared down the hall.

Françoise sighed and crossed her arms. "It's a vacation cottage Papa inherited a few years ago. Near Toulouse. Papa loves it there, so that's probably the home he was talking about in the cipher."

Drake nodded. "Let's go." He pulled my arm and motioned his men to join him. "The girl might be lying."

"So what do we do with her?" Agent Fullerton asked.

"Simple." Drake flashed a wide grin. "We take her with us."

31

THE UPSIDE: THEY DIDN'T HIT US IN THE

head. Considering that I already had three sizable bumps at various points on my scalp, that was a huge plus. Downside: I got to sit next to Françoise, who kept kicking me in the shins with her heels. Drake took off in his fancy car, leaving us with a small rental.

"You helped him?" She shook her head and looked at me with such hate in her eyes, I thought she might actually light me on fire. "Do you know who he is?"

"Your uncle, apparently." We were in the back of the red car that had followed me from the airport, with Agent Fullerton driving and French Bad Guy riding shotgun. I think the only reason they didn't toss us both in the trunk was because it was a compact, and there wasn't room for two. "Drake is American?"

"By choice, yes." Françoise sighed. "He and Papa went to America for one of those college foreign exchange programs. Only Jules never came back to France. Papa told me they had a fight over what to do with the Vault, and then they lost touch. Until he came over for dinner last week.

"Uncle Jules changed his last name to Drake, so he would sound more American—and he basically abandoned the Mégère family." Françoise shook her head in anger. "And now he's back. I should have known it was him. All he wants is money."

"He's the one who kidnapped your father, you know," I whispered. "He told me earlier, when he still thought I was Ben."

Françoise clenched her fists.

"We'll get him back," I said.

The car came to an abrupt stop, and I realized I hadn't been paying attention to see where we were going. Agent Fullerton turned around and gave us both a glare. "Get out, and no running. You run, you die—got it?"

We both nodded. When I got out, I realized we were at the Charles de Gaulle airport rental car drop-off.

Agent Fullerton went inside the office to return the key while French Bad Guy waited outside with us.

"How are you going to fly us out like this?" I lifted my tied hands.

"We've got a private jet." French Bad Guy kept looking

around, like someone might jump him at any moment.

"He can afford a private jet, and you're driving a compact rental car?" I fake laughed to Françoise, who just looked away. She'd obviously never talked her way out of a jam before. "The boss gets a Mercedes," I went on to the French dude, "and you get a . . . what?"

"A compact rental," the guy said, but I'd gotten his attention.

"What's your name?"

The guy squinted, and then he smiled. "You can call me Bob."

"Bob, okay. You're Drake's right-hand man, aren't you?" I stepped a little closer, and nodded toward the rental office. "I mean, your partner, Agent Fullerton, isn't a bad guy, but he's obviously not the brains of the operation. Right?"

Bob straightened his shoulders. "Right."

"And let's face it: it's only a matter of time before he stabs you in the back."

"You should be quiet," Bob said, but he didn't mean it, I could tell.

"A rental car is for small-timers. That's not you." I shrugged. "I'm just saying."

I was glad Bob didn't see Françoise roll her eyes. Agent Fullerton came out of the rental car building and folded some euros into his back pocket. "Let's go."

They had us each walk between them, so there was no way we could run. Not that I would. I had to save Françoise and her dad. We navigated the Parisian airport, rushing until we came to a gate marked *Privé*.

There were about four small planes outside on the brightly lit tarmac. Where were Agent Stark and Albert Black? Wasn't anyone missing one twelve-year-old Benjamin Green lookalike, also known as Chicken Boy?

"This way!" Agent Fullerton pulled Françoise roughly by her sleeve. I followed past the pretty, shiny white airplanes until we saw Drake's Mercedes in front of a rusted old plane that had a faded picture of the Eiffel Tower on it. Drake was on his phone, looking like he was about to blow up. "This is unacceptable! I reserved a private plane, not a rust bucket. What do you mean my second payment didn't go through? Check again!" Then after a pause, to his bad guys, "Get them on the plane!"

We walked the rickety little ladder and ducked our heads to get inside. "Get in the back." Bob pushed his fingers hard into my backpack, so hard I could feel it ram into my spine. The plane was very dimly lit. I walked slowly so I wouldn't trip over any of the seats.

But then Françoise pushed me aside and rushed toward the back of the plane. "Papa!"

Jacques Mégère looked tired and his hair was sticking up even more than in the picture Agent Stark had shown me. He kept hugging Françoise, and it wasn't until I sat down in the seat across from them that she let go and wiped her eyes.

"Are you all right, Papa?" Françoise studied his face and all the rest of him anxiously. "Did they hurt you?"

Jacques shook his head and gave her a tired smile. "I'm

fine, my sweetie pie. Jules is still my brother. He won't hurt me."

"Lousy brother if you ask me," Françoise muttered. "Does he really expect you to reveal the location of the da Vinci collection? The Dangerous Double?"

"He says all he wants is the evil *Mona Lisa*. I say no." Another tired smile. "But now he has found you and . . . this boy." Jacques turned his attention to me. "He looks like Benjamin, the boy from the bakery who brought me here."

"His name is Linc," Françoise said, and then she surprised me by adding, "He's a friend."

Jacques touched Françoise's face. "Why are you here?"

Françoise went on to tell him about us following his codes and ciphers, how Drake was right on our tail, and how his guys had come to the bakery. Meanwhile, I looked around for our bad guy duo, hoping that maybe we'd have a chance to escape. But they stood near the open door. I could faintly hear Drake yelling outside, still trying to get a better plane.

"Mom," Jacques muttered. "Jules wouldn't hurt her, would he? Is she all right?"

"Grandma is fine, don't worry." Françoise smiled. "I thought she was going to smack Uncle Jules with a stick."

Jacques laughed, but his smile quickly faded. "I should have known this day would come. Jules wants his piece of the pie. He already has several potential buyers for the painting, you know. Terrorists."

"Doesn't Uncle Jules care that they'll use the painting's powers to kill?"

Jacques just gave her a sad smile and a little shrug. "Money," he said. "Jules always wanted a fortune, and soon he'll have it."

Jacques was about to say more, but Drake stepped onto the plane. "Well, little brother, I guess this is the moment of truth. I found your secret hiding place—did you think I wouldn't be able to?"

Jacques looked confused.

"The vacation home in Toulouse," Françoise said, giving her father an urgent stare. "Uncle Jules figured out that you were talking about that home in your cipher on the Moulin de la Galette menu."

"Ah," Jacques said in a sad tone. "You have outsmarted me, Jules."

Drake looked smug. "And once I have the evil *Mona Lisa*, I will have no need for these two annoying little kids. Or you," he said to Jacques, waving his gun.

Jacques slumped in his seat.

"It's time for the secret Vault collection to be out for the world to enjoy. And for me to profit."

32

DRAKE MADE ANOTHER CALL. AFTER
yelling to the poor person on the other end, he threw his
phone across the plane. Then he took a deep breath. "Let's
GO!" he yelled at his bad guys in the back.

Bob gave Agent Fullerton a dirty look, but then settled
into the seat near us.

"You, go find my phone," Drake said to Bob. "I think I
tossed it somewhere over there." He motioned toward the
middle of the plane, under some seats. The plane began to
rumble, and the engines made a very high-pitched sound,
one that couldn't be healthy in my opinion.

Bob was scrambling on the floor for Drake's phone,
when the plane moved and made a sharp right turn. He

cursed in French as he whacked his head against one of the seats. Vindication, I thought as I touched my head where the big bumps were throbbing. As Bob got up, clutching Drake's phone, I mouthed the words: *compact rental car.*

The plane picked up speed, and sent Bob flying. The phone jumped from his hand, disappearing between the seats again.

Agent Fullerton laughed. "Sit, you fool."

But Bob was scrambling for the phone, cursing louder now, and pointing at Agent Fullerton.

I sat back, holding tight during takeoff. My backpack was by my feet. The stickers—without the tracking device, they were no use, but I figured they might help us if Henry could build a new tracker. Jacques's jacket was draped over the chair next to me. While everyone was focused on Bob's angry tirade, I pulled an I Love Paris sticker from my backpack. And slapped it onto Jacques's inside pocket.

Bob was at the back of the plane, obviously ready to take a stand. "I am keeping this," he said, waving the phone while walking toward the front.

"Give me the phone." Drake got up.

"You will not get it until you apologize. I am your right-hand man, the brains of the operation, yet you treat me like a fool."

"Because you *are* a fool. Give me my phone and sit down." Drake pointed to the empty seats behind me and Françoise. "By the children." He laughed, and Agent Fullerton joined in.

"You think I'm a joke." Bob clenched his jaw as he got

closer. I glanced around. The exit door was at the front of the plane. "You think I'm a doll you can manipulate," Bob cried.

"You mean a puppet?" Drake said with a scowl. "You really need to work on your English."

But then Bob pushed Drake and tossed the phone down, crushing it under his big black boot with a satisfied look on his face. "Who is the puppet now, huh?"

Suddenly, everything happened at once: the plane dropped due to turbulence, Drake fumbled for his gun, and Agent Fullerton went after Bob.

I knew this was our chance. Françoise saw it, too, because she got up and pulled her father along to the front of the plane.

I grabbed my backpack and followed. Agent Fullerton, Bob, and Drake were fighting in the rear of the plane, but I knew that wouldn't last much longer—they would figure out we were trying to escape.

Françoise gave me a look of terror. "There are no parachutes."

"I have one inside my backpack," I said, making a mental note to thank Henry.

"But there are three of us!" Françoise said, almost in tears. "Now what?"

I had no good answer, but Françoise's father did. "You kids go. If you hold on to Lincoln, he'll get you down safe."

"No, Papa, we came here for you." Françoise clutched his arm.

Jacques Mégère shook his head. He handed Françoise

a wooden box, which she stuffed inside her jacket pocket. "You must go," Jacques said. "I'll be fine—Jules is my brother. I know how to handle him." He lifted the giant red lever, opened the door, and stepped aside, bracing himself so he wouldn't fall.

I strapped on my backpack, took Françoise's hand, and felt, really, really sick all of a sudden. "I can't do this." Jumping out of an airplane—that was Benjamin Green's territory. And I knew by now that pretending to be the guy only got me into more trouble.

"Of course you can," Jacques said. "Remember: just follow the cipher."

And he pushed us both out of the plane.

33

I COULDN'T BREATHE, THINK, OR ANY-

thing. *I was flying!* Actually, forget that—*I was falling!*

This was not good.

Françoise seemed oddly calm next to me as we plunged through the white clouds. Toward the lights of Paris.

I was going to die. We could fall right on top of a building! Splatter on the French pavement or something. Mom would have to come and scrape me up, and—

Then I thought of the parachute in my backpack. "My chute!" I yelled, trying to grab behind me, lifting the flap to the cord.

Françoise hugged me, which confused me at first. Let's

be honest: yesterday, the girl had been ready to choke me with a stick. But then she just yanked the cord, and we both jerked back as the parachute opened to slow our descent.

And it was very peaceful all of a sudden. The clouds cleared, and we had a fantastic view of Paris. The way the main streets fanned out like a star, with all the bright lights—it was breathtaking. And so was the thin air: I felt pretty dizzy as we made our way down.

"Hold on to me," Françoise said as she put my arms around her waist. She pulled the chute, guiding us toward the Eiffel Tower, and then to the fountain in front of it.

We hit the water, and Françoise let go of me. I rolled, rolled, rolled, until I was wrapped inside the parachute like a cocoon.

"Help?" I asked, trying to see through the white fabric. "Françoise?" She'd pulled another one of her disappearing acts. Where had she gone so fast?

The water was freezing. I heard footsteps all around me. When I finally stuck my head through a hole in my parachute package, I looked right at three faces.

Very angry policemen's faces.

"Bonjour?" I tried a friendly smile.

The French police didn't smile back. Instead, I was arrested, for the third time in two days. Mrs. Valdez would be shocked by how I'd taken the getting-into-trouble thing to a whole new and international level.

Thankfully, Albert Black showed up to pass cigars to the police and crack jokes in French.

Agent Stark helped me roll up the wet parachute. "Is there anything you can do without getting into trouble? Never mind." She shook her head. "Don't answer that."

The French police tore up the ticket. They could be nice when you had a big guy with Cuban cigars and a top secret badge on your side.

I kept looking around for Françoise, but no dice. Still, I couldn't blame my partner in crime for not waiting around to get arrested.

People had crowded near the fountain, trying to see if I was going to be dragged away in handcuffs like on TV, but eventually, they took off. So did Agent Stark, after telling me to keep out of trouble, "and get cleaned up."

"You just had to use that parachute, didn't you?" Albert Black said with a sigh as we started back to the hotel.

"Why else did Henry give me one?" I got into a cab.

Sitting back in his seat, Albert Black said, "So tell me what happened—the short version."

I told Black that Agent Fullerton was sabotaging the mission, and how we had to jump from the plane to get away. "And Drake is Jacques Mégère's brother."

Albert Black chewed on that as our cabdriver navigated Paris's nighttime traffic. "So now Drake is getting the *Mona Lisa* somewhere in Toulouse?" Black asked.

"That was Françoise. She tricked him into thinking that her dad hid it at the family vacation home."

He laughed. "That girl would make a mighty fine agent, kid. Now when you were on the plane, did Mégère tell you where he put the evil *Mona Lisa*?"

I shook my head. "He just said to follow the cipher, which says it's at home. *Home sweet home.* Whatever that means."

Albert Black sighed. "We're running out of time here, Linc. That mother of yours is calling all over the place, trying to find out if boot camp will let you come home for Thanksgiving, and if you're eating enough."

"That sounds like Mom all right. I'll call home and see if I can get her to cut it out."

Albert Black touched my shoulder, and shook his head. "I'm closing this case."

"Why?"

"The boss's orders."

"Ah."

"We're not exactly undercover here, with you getting into it with the French police every day ."

I thought of arguing that the first arrest was my own fault for trying to skateboard to the arc, but the second time it was Ben's doing, and the third time Drake's. And that it was a good thing I escaped, otherwise I might be chopped into small pieces right about now. But I knew Albert had made up his mind. "What about Ben?"

Albert shrugged. "Had to let the kid go. Long story."

"Long story?" The cab pulled up to the Princesse, and the driver glanced in his rearview mirror, hinting that our time was up.

"It's almost ten. Time to call it a day," Albert Black said. He handed the driver a euro bill, and we both got out.

"So that's it?" I couldn't believe the mission was over. "How about my family, the lawsuit?"

"It'll be taken care of. You have my word."

"Even without the evil—"

"Shhh." Albert Black cut me off. "Yes. Now get some sleep. We're flying out of here tomorrow at three, Linc. Make sure you're ready when the cab comes at noon." He smacked my shoulder.

"Sure. Yeah."

"Tomorrow, you can go say good-bye to the girl, all right? And bring us back a few of the croissants with the chocolate in the middle. I like those."

34

PLACE: MY COMFY HOTEL BED

TIME: THURSDAY, 1:59 A.M.

STATUS: ABOUT TO BE RUDELY AWAKENED

NOW THAT THE GOVERNMENT PROMISED to take care of the Baker lawsuit troubles, you'd think I was done, right?

Think again. I mean, Drake's guys weren't just going to give up, I should've known that. Not with five hundred million dollars at stake. But I didn't think about this—I was just sleeping like a bear. I mean, all that excitement had worn me out.

So when my phone rang I didn't even open my eyes to look at the number on the little caller ID screen. I just picked up and cleared my throat. "Hello?"

"Hello, Lincoln Baker." The voice on the line sounded dark and very awake.

"Who's this?" I sat up, blinking at the clock. "You know it's two in the morning?"

"It's five in the afternoon here in California. Sunny, warm."

My stomach dropped. I checked my phone's screen. This creep was calling from my house.

"It's a beautiful day for a last-minute doctor's appointment."

"Who is this?" I was wide-awake now.

"Today, I'm Dave from D.E. Health Services. Those initials stand for Drake Enterprises, in case you're wondering. Your mother was so grateful we could fit your grandfather in for his hearing-aid appointment."

"You took Grandpa?" My voice was squeaky.

"Just for a few hours. I have a message from Drake."

I tried to swallow, but I couldn't.

"Bring him the evil *Mona Lisa*." The guy paused. "And I'll be sure to bring your grandpa home safely."

"But I don't have it."

"I'm just the messenger. Oh, and there's another part to the message."

I waited, too terrified to talk.

"Don't tell the police or your top secret friends, or else."

He didn't need to say more. "And happy Thanksgiving."

"Leave my grandpa alone!" I yelled, but the line was dead.

You know that part in the story where you think it couldn't possibly get any worse, but it does? This was that point. Only this wasn't some movie.

I got up and paced my room, tripping over my backpack, cursing. Grandpa had been captured by the bad guys as I slept in my Paris hotel room. All this time I'd spent trying to save my family, and look where it got us.

Would they hurt Grandpa? I mean, he was a ninja in the way he snuck up on you, but he's also eighty-three. His ninja skills could only take him so far.

I sat down on my bed, took a deep breath, and forced myself to focus. There wasn't time for me to freak out; I had to stay calm.

I thought of calling Daryl or Sam, but that wouldn't work. I couldn't tell them about the message. Not that they'd believe me anyway, and besides, their parents weren't too crazy about my Linc disasters. Which left me only one option.

I had to find the evil *Mona Lisa*.

I couldn't do anything right then—I mean, it was two in the morning. I at least had to wait for France to wake up. So I spent hours tossing and turning in my now-not-comfy-anymore bed. Thinking of Grandpa. Drake. What was I supposed to do now?

At seven, I took a thirty-second shower and rushed out the door. When I got onto the elevator, I used my room key card and pushed the P button. I needed help.

I needed my friend Henry. And knowing him, he was already hard at work on the next genius gadget.

When I got to the Penthouse floor, the elevator opened to a cluttered room. There were boxes everywhere and a few suitcases. Henry was taping up a box at the dining room table. "Hey, Linc." He frowned when I got closer. "Dude, you don't look so good."

I glanced around, to see if any of the agents were there to hear us. "I need your help with something." I told Henry about the phone call, how the guy had kidnapped my grandpa, and how I needed to give Drake the evil *Mona Lisa*.

"I think I can help you." Henry ripped the tape off one of the boxes and dug inside. "Do you remember that device I was working on?"

"The evil detector, something about heat sensing or whatever?"

"I call it the Double Detector." Henry pulled what looked like a tablet computer from the box. "It looks ordinary, right?" He turned the Double Detector on, and there was a picture of the latest kid-wizard novel. "Looks like I'm reading the new bestseller, right? But not if I punch this blue button four times, like this."

We both waited, until the book cover changed to a blue screen.

"Now what?"

Henry bit his lip. "Well, now we need a Dangerous Double. When you get this detector near the evil *Mona Lisa*, it will register the painting's temperature to be twenty point two degrees Celsius. You'll see it as a red rectangle on your screen."

"Can you show me?"

"Not without the painting. And if we had that, we wouldn't be talking." Henry turned the Double Detector off. "I tested it on a cup of water at exactly twenty point two Celsius—but we don't have time to heat water now. Get within twenty feet of the evil *Mona Lisa* and it'll work."

"Thanks." I tucked the Double Detector into my backpack.

"You want me to come?" Henry pushed his glasses up, but I knew he was just more comfortable in a lab.

"I'll be fine." I turned and punched the elevator call button. The doors opened right away, like it knew I had no time to waste. I got on, taking a deep breath.

"Hey, Linc," Henry called from his stack of boxes, just as the doors began to close. "Don't forget: you can always use the Henry!"

35

AS I RODE THE ELEVATOR DOWN FROM the Penthouse, I tried to come up with a plan to find the evil *Mona Lisa*. I mean, the Double Detector was useful only if I was within twenty feet of the painting. Paris is a big city, right? And this new clue wasn't exactly easy to interpret.

Home sweet home. Could mean lots of things. I really needed Françoise's help. So I took off on my skateboard across Paris, rushing to make it to the Mégère bakery.

Françoise's grandma was outside on the sidewalk, sweeping up bits of glass. The place looked even worse in daylight, with all the windows broken by Drake, a forgotten bread basket strewn in the street. I picked it up and waved to Françoise's grandma. She gave me a cranky look as I grabbed my skateboard and went inside.

Françoise was cleaning up the mess in the store. There was an open trash bag full of crushed pastries, mashed chocolates, and pieces of bread—Mégère creations that Drake and his guys had trampled over.

"Runaway basket," I said, stepping over broken glass to place it on the counter.

"Hey," Françoise said with a little smile. "I see you managed to get out of your parachute."

"The police showed up. They were super helpful." I took off my backpack, attached my skateboard to it with Henry's nifty Velcro straps, and brushed some glass aside to set it in a corner. "I really have to find the evil *Mona Lisa*," I blurted out. I told Françoise about the phone call, Grandpa being kidnapped, everything. "We have to solve this last clue, for both our families."

"What happens after we find the evil *Mona Lisa*?"

"You get your dad back, I get Grandpa." But then I realized why she asked me her question. "And Drake sells the evil *Mona Lisa* to this terrorist group."

Françoise nodded in silence.

"We'll just have to improvise. Chase Drake and the painting down or something."

"Sure, that's a great plan."

"What was in the box your father gave you on the airplane?" I asked, hoping to change the subject.

She reached inside her jacket and pulled out the rectangular wooden box. Françoise opened it, and carefully picked up these wire-rimmed glasses. "They were stored with the secret da Vinci collection."

"What makes these so special?"

"You use them so you can look at the painting and not get hypnotized—they're just a really strong prescription that makes it hard to see. The story was that da Vinci's assistant Salai stole the glasses from a neighbor. He was a bit of a thief, I guess." Françoise closed the box and tucked it back inside her jacket. "We have to be close to the painting for Papa to give me these."

"I still don't get where that cipher on the menu was trying to get us to go."

"Could your decoding have been wrong?" Françoise put a couple of baskets back on the shelf.

"*Home sweet home*—there's nothing else it could be." I pictured the menu inside my head. "The cipher circled the dessert menu, around and around."

"Around and around," Françoise mumbled, looking at the window display.

We looked at each other, and both yelled the answer at the same time, "The pie!" We rushed over to the display window, where the fake pie was still spinning on the turntable.

"So what's the story on this thing?" I asked. It looked just like a real apple pie. But when you stepped closer, you could see it was kind of shiny and waxy. Definitely a fake.

"Mama gave it to Papa as a birthday present. She had a local artist make it," Françoise said. "It was one of the last things she did before she died. My parents met here in the bakery when Mama came in for an apple pie." She lifted the pie, then showed the bottom to me with a triumphant smile. "Our next code!"

Here's what we saw:

BCOVUT

AKFAL

I studied the letters. "Yeah, this makes zero sense."

Françoise pulled out *Codes and Ciphers.* "It could be a lot of different things." She flipped the pages, shook her head a few times. "Wait—write the words on a piece of paper, one above the other, with more space between the letters.

"Now connect the letters, zigzagging from the top to the bottom, and back." She showed me the codebook. "It's a rail fence cipher, see?"

I grabbed a notebook from the counter and did like she said. We found our next answer.

36

THURSDAY, 9:30 A.M.

    BCOVUT

    AKFAL

"IT SAYS, 'BACK OF VAULT.' BUT ISN'T IT
empty?" I looked at Françoise.

"Let's find out." She put the pie back onto its carousel.
Outside, Françoise's grandma was leaning on her broom,
talking to another old lady.

We hurried downstairs, Françoise fumbling with her
keys, both of us dying to know what was next. Could the evil
Mona Lisa still be at the bakery?

A waft of cold air welcomed us to the Vault. We slowed,

looking at the empty racks and the big wooden desk and the empty wooden bookcases behind it.

The desk looked the same, but I glanced underneath it, to see if maybe there was a piece of paper taped to the bottom. Or maybe there was a secret drawer, like you see in the movies. Then I started pushing the bookshelves to see if they'd move. "Help me," I said to Françoise.

The empty bookcases were surprisingly easy to slide away. But behind them there was no wall, just a big, black hole.

"It's a tunnel," I said.

"He did it! I can't believe it!" Françoise pushed ahead of me, crawling into the darkness.

I didn't share her excitement. I'm really not into darkness and closed-in spaces, and my time in that rental car trunk didn't help. "You have a flashlight?" I called from the tunnel opening. It was wide enough for a person, and definitely easy to crawl through, but it was pitch-dark.

Then I saw a light, coming from ten feet or so ahead.

"Come on!" Françoise called.

"All right." The dirt was cold and wet, so I crawled fast, until the tunnel widened.

Into a cave that smelled like sulfur. Françoise was moving around in a hurry, lighting candles with matches that I guessed her father left behind. "Look!" she pointed to my left. The cave was still really dark and, from what I could tell, about the size of our house. It was hard to see in the flickering candlelight, but not so hard that I couldn't make out old crates, big and small, stacked along the wall. "So this is where your dad put the secret da Vinci collection? He dug a cave?"

"No, he just dug the tunnel to the Vault." Françoise lit another candle, smiling. "He used to talk about it: digging to connect the Vault to the cave and the tunnel system. But then he stopped, and I thought he dropped the idea."

"Apparently he bought a bigger shovel." I moved around the da Vinci artifacts. It just looked like a heap of old crates that might be in someone's garage. "Is the Dangerous Double here?" I whispered.

"I don't see the box." Françoise joined me near the collection, shaking her head. "And Papa wouldn't have taken it out of the box—it would be too dangerous."

"So where is the evil *Mona Lisa*?" I was getting frustrated now—my grandpa's life was on the line, and this Mégère dude was having us play games to get the painting.

"Shhhh!" Françoise punched my arm and pointed to another very narrow tunnel on the other side. "It's illegal to come down here. The police arrest cataphiles on sight."

"Great. The police here in Paris love me already. What are cataphiles?"

"Those who explore the catacombs," she said with pride.

"Couldn't some cataphile take this da Vinci collection?"

"It doesn't look like much, and most people don't know where the tunnels are." She continued lighting candles so we could see better.

"There are tunnels under all Paris? So that's how you kept disappearing."

Françoise nodded. "The better part of the city is over the tunnels."

"Who dug these, anyway?"

"These used to be quarries. It's where they got the stone to build Roman houses, and later, Nôtre Dame. The last time I came here was with my mother, before she died," Françoise said, her voice trailing off. "Papa must've left a clue down here."

Once all the candles were lit, I could see a giant mural on the walls. It looked like one of those creative interpretations of a map—like the kind they give you at Disneyland. There was the Eiffel Tower, the Arc de Triomphe, Nôtre Dame and Sacré Coeur, and some other buildings I didn't recognize. And the Mégère bakery, under a bright pink sky and a very big yellow sun. There was a dragon underneath the city with eyes like smoldering fire.

"My mother made this mural." Françoise ran her hands along the brightly colored scene. "She let me paint the sun." She stepped close to the wall of the cave, and pointed to a small drawing of a cat inside a big triangle of a building. "That's the pyramid part of the Louvre—my mother painted it. But this cat is not her work. The drawing is too simple."

She was right. Whoever did it wasn't much of an artist, let me tell you. Here's what it looked like:

"It could be a message from your dad." It looked like whoever painted the picture was four years old or in a hurry. "What is *NW*?"

Françoise pulled out her *Codes and Ciphers* book. It didn't take her long to find the answer. "The picture of the cat could be a hobo sign."

"A what?"

"A hobo sign. Homeless people who used the railroads sent messages to each other with these. The signs would tell other hoboes if it was a good place to be, if there were cops around—that sort of thing."

"So what—there's a cat in the Louvre?"

37

"A PICTURE OF A CAT MEANS 'A KIND lady lives here' the book claims," Françoise said. "I don't know who that is, but maybe that lady has our next clue."

"You think maybe the *N* and *W* are her initials?"

"Maybe. Whatever it means, we have to go to the Louvre." Françoise rushed around the cave, blowing out the candles, before she went through the tunnel that led back to the Vault. I had to rush to catch up with her, or I would be left in the dark. Literally.

"Should we bring your da Vinci collection back into the Vault?" I asked. That stuff had to be worth millions.

Françoise hesitated, but shook her head. "It's safer where it is right now."

"Do you think this kind lady at the Louvre is a friend of your father's?" I asked as we pushed the bookcases back to cover the tunnel entrance. "Do you know anybody he might know, like somebody with the initials *NW*?"

"I don't think so," Françoise answered. I followed her out of the Vault.

"Norah or Natalie or something?"

"No. I don't know, okay?"

As we came upstairs to the bakery, I was grateful for the daylight. This underground tunnel system was really cool and adventurous, but there was something to be said for being able to breathe fresh air. Françoise's grandma was still outside, busy talking to some guys in uniform, there to replace the glass.

"Let's get to the Louvre," Françoise said, tossing me my backpack. Dad's compass knocked against my arm.

Then I thought of something. "What if *NW* aren't initials?" I said, pulling Françoise's arm. "What if it's a location, like on a compass?"

"Northwest?"

"Yeah."

Françoise thought about that for a moment. "I guess we'll start at the northwest part of the Louvre."

"Now we're getting somewhere." I was feeling pretty smart right about then.

Françoise took off from the Mégère bakery at her usual

fast pace, and I was glad I had my skateboard at the ready. Together, we almost knocked a few tourists off their feet, but we made it to the Louvre by eleven.

Eleven o'clock. I was supposed to be at the Princesse in an hour, packed and ready to go home. I pictured Albert Black, waiting by the cab to take us to the airport. He'd be seriously miffed.

My compass knocked against my back, reminding me why I was here.

Find the evil *Mona Lisa*. Save Grandpa. Françoise and I were so close, I could feel it. That cab would just have to wait.

The Louvre Museum was a big palace. The U-shaped building looked a lot like someone had taken a bunch of mansions and lined them up, with a large plaza and a fountain. There was a statue of a guy on a horse, and behind it, a glass pyramid that looked totally out of place. The entry was busy with tourists, lining up to get inside the museum.

We stood in line for a while to get inside the pyramid. First, we took an escalator down to the giant lobby, which was crammed full of people, almost as bad as the chickens in the barn at the Johnson farm.

Françoise rushed to this machine where she bought us both a ticket before I could give her money. Security made me turn in my backpack and skateboard, but I managed to tuck the Double Detector in my cargo pants' pocket.

I turned around and tried to keep up with Françoise as she rushed down a hall in an ocean of tourists. Apparently, she knew where she was going.

But then I heard a voice in the crowd that chilled me like the Lompoc morning fog.

"Over here!"

It was Drake. "Françoise, Lincoln!" He stood there with his arms spread wide, like he was oh so happy to see us.

Françoise froze.

"These are my children, finally!" Drake said over his shoulder. There was a tour guide and about a dozen tourists, looking impatient. "Come, children." He wrapped his arms around our shoulders, clamping me tight with his evil fingers.

I was stuck.

Drake let go of me and pretended to look for something in his jacket's inside breast pocket. "I have a knife pointed right at the girl," he hissed in my ear. "You move, she's dead."

38

I SWALLOWED. FRANÇOISE STOOD FROZEN.
I wanted to reach over and punch her uncle for arranging Grandpa's abduction. But I couldn't. Not while he had Françoise at knifepoint.

"I need that painting," Drake hissed. "My buyer is coming for it at one o'clock. I have to deliver."

"Or what?" I was dumb enough to ask.

"Or I'm dead. But you will go first." In other words: we were stuck playing along with this crazy man.

My phone rang.

"Turn that off!" The tour guide lady snapped. Definitely not the nice lady we were hoping to find.

I silenced the phone. It was probably Agent Stark or

213

Albert Black, wondering why I wasn't at the hotel. Or maybe it was that bad guy who had Grandpa. I itched to know.

Françoise and I followed along with Drake at the back of the group. "Did you really think I wouldn't find you here?" he hissed into Françoise's ear. "Did you think I was stupid enough to believe your story about the vacation home after you abandoned your father on the plane? You know, it wasn't difficult to figure the evil *Mona Lisa* might be hidden here. Jacques always liked to play games, and what better way to hide something than in plain sight."

Françoise was silent.

"I know my brother," Drake added with a smug smile.

"Now we move onwaaaard . . ." Tour Guide Lady droned on. You could tell she did this tour something like a hundred times a day, because she sounded like a robot.

"So where is it, hmmmm?" Drake hissed in my ear now.

"I don't know," I said loudly. "I'm just here for the tour, man, so shhhh." That got me a jab from his gnarly elbow.

"Monsieur," Tour Guide Lady called with a sourpuss face, eyebrows raised. "Please keep your children quiet." Some irritated tour people added a dirty glare.

"Yes, mademoiselle," Drake said with a smile.

I glanced around the big room full of fancy oil paintings. There were guards at both doors, sensors for the paintings. I could reach over and pull one of the paintings down or something, but that would just get me arrested. Then Drake would pretend he was my dad, and we'd be right back where we started.

I needed a diversion.

"And here we have the painting everyone wants to see: the *Mona Lisa*," Tour Guide Lady said. "She is also known as la Joconde and was painted in the sixteenth century by the famous Leonardo da Vinci."

I felt Drake perk up. "There she is," he mumbled, mesmerized by the small painting behind the glass shield. This was it? The painting was so small. We moved closer, which wasn't easy. Dozens of tourists were crammed around it.

"The lady is missing her eyebrows. It is believed that hundreds of years ago, someone attempted to clean the painting and accidentally rubbed them off." That got some mumbling from our tour group. "In 2005, the *Mona Lisa* was given her own room—as you can see, she needs her space." Tour Guide Lady chuckled at her own joke.

Drake licked his lips. "Is that it? Did my brother swap this *Mona Lisa* with the evil one from the Vault?" he hissed in Françoise's ear. But she didn't respond.

Not that she had to. It didn't take a genius to figure out that with all the security surrounding the *Mona Lisa*, it was impossible to get near her, let alone swap it with another painting. And there were no hypnotized, homicidal people floating around the Louvre.

I didn't need my Double Detector to know that this wasn't the evil *Mona Lisa*.

But Drake lingered anyway, even when our tour moved along. "What did you do, Jacques . . . ?"

"Why don't you ask *him*?" I said, still desperately looking for a way out. I needed some sort of commotion so Françoise and I could make a run for it. "Don't you still have your brother chained to a chair somewhere?"

Drake tensed up next to me, digging his fingers even deeper into my flesh.

And I realized, "Jacques Mégère got away, didn't he?"

Drake didn't answer, but his expression confirmed my suspicions. This was good—now Drake didn't have that to threaten Françoise with anymore. Françoise perked up.

"How about my grandpa, huh?" I asked just a little too loud.

"And we move along," Tour Guide Lady squawked near the doorway, giving me the evil eye. "I know she can be hypnotizing, but it's time to go. You can always buy a nice reproduction in our gift shop."

You have no idea how hypnotizing she can really be, lady, I wanted to say. But Tour Guide Lady was right about one thing: it was time to go. I looked at her and at the doorway she stood in.

And I had an idea of something I could do, a lever I could pull. One I'd wanted to pull my whole life—and you know you've always wanted to do it, too. This was no chicken farm, and this lever wouldn't send feathers flying, but it sure would give Françoise and me a chance to get free.

I pushed away from Drake, rushed across the room.

And I couldn't help but smile at Tour Guide Lady when I reached out for the red lever and pulled the fire alarm.

39

THE NOISE WAS LIKE AN EXPLOSION
happened. Screaming. A wailing alarm. People were shouting and pushing. Gates crashing down to protect the paintings—I had unleashed chaos in the Louvre. This was a new kind of crazy, even for me. But there was no time to stand around to admire my Linc disaster, much as I wanted to. Françoise pulled away from Drake, and without saying a word, we both ran. I didn't look back as we rushed through halls filled with confused people. I could only hope that we were faster than Drake. It was time to scram.

"This way," Françoise said, rushing to the right, until we came to the spiral staircase. We hurried down and back up again on the escalator, pushing past people where we could. "Come on!"

As we left the glass pyramid, I saw Drake down below, getting on the escalator. "Don't stop running!" I yelled at Françoise. "He's right behind us!" It took all my strength just to keep up with Françoise.

"Come on!" she called over her shoulder, taking one of the side streets.

I looked back and couldn't see Drake. But I knew he had to be right on our heels. We raced down the Paris streets. The cobblestones made me trip a few times, but I didn't stop. Honestly, I knew that if I did, I'd lose Françoise.

After what seemed like forever, she reached a manhole cover that she lifted with ease. The tunnels, of course! I followed her down into the hole and covered it as fast as I could. Then we made our way down the metal ladder and into the tunnel, where Françoise finally slowed down. Which was a good thing. My lungs were exploding.

"Do you think he saw us?" I asked, breathing heavy.

Françoise seemed unaffected by our sprint out of the Louvre and through central Paris. She shrugged. "Only if he's fast."

I nodded and followed her down the tunnel. "Where are we going?"

She stopped. "I don't know. I suppose we can simply wait here awhile for my uncle to leave."

"And go back?"

"The painting is there, I'm sure of it now." Her eyes were

like fire, like the dragon painting in the cave. "The evil *Mona Lisa* is somewhere in the museum we're not thinking of. Maybe it's this kind lady who knows where the painting is."

And suddenly, I remembered something from our tour. "Do you remember what the tour guide said?"

Françoise gave me a look. "I wasn't exactly paying attention. The knife was more pressing."

I felt great. See, I may not look like I'm learning much when I'm in class or on a field trip or on a tour of the Louvre with a bad guy—but I do. Stuff seeps into my brain anyway. Like that offhanded joke the tour guide had made. "She said that you can buy a reproduction, a fake version of the paintings, in the gift shop."

Françoise's face lit up. "That would be the kind of thing Papa would do: hide it in plain sight. Just like my uncle said."

"So where is the gift shop?"

"There are several," Françoise said. "But for the replicas, you have to go to the lobby under the glass pyramid, on the lower ground floor. Wait—that's on the northwest side of the pyramid," she said with a grin.

We hurried out of the tunnel and up to the surface.

"Look," I said as we made our way through Paris. I pulled the Double Detector from my cargo pants' pocket. "Henry made a gadget that can detect the evil *Mona Lisa*."

"The twenty point two degree temperature," Françoise said, nodding. I should've known—she'd read the da Vinci notebooks, too.

"You two should get together sometime," I mumbled. "All

we need to do is get within twenty feet. So once we're inside the gift shop, it should be easy to find the evil *Mona Lisa*."

We made our way back to the giant Louvre central courtyard, going against the flow of tourists. The fire alarm stunt I'd pulled had probably changed their plans for the day.

"Watch out!" I pulled Françoise's sleeve as I saw him: Drake, scanning the crowd for his precious children.

We used the clusters of tourists to hide and get closer to the museum. Sometimes being a kid comes in mighty handy: you're short, and everyone assumes you belong to the adult you stand closest to.

"Let's sneak in," Françoise said once we reached the pyramid entrance to the Louvre.

But a guard stopped us in our tracks. "There are no visitors allowed in the museum," he said matter-of-factly. "There was a fire alarm."

"We lost our parents, and now we're trying to find them," Françoise said with a smile. She could be pretty nice and sweet when she wanted to be.

"There are no visitors inside," the guard simply said, pointing at the plaza that stretched to the other side of the pyramid. "They're probably out here somewhere." This wasn't going to work.

Françoise nodded.

And then I saw him: Benjamin Green. He was propping open a door on the far end of the southern wall, motioning for us to come inside.

Like he was our ally.

40

NO, THANKS. I WOULDN'T TRUST BEN-
jamin Green if he was the last person on earth.

"Hey, isn't that Benjamin Green?" Françoise asked me, poking my ribs. The door was still cracked open a little. "Is he keeping it open for us?"

I pulled her arm, since she seemed ready to run on over. "What if this is a trap? Why would we trust this guy?"

Françoise motioned at the guard. "We don't have too many other options, do we?"

All right, so she had a point, much as I hated to admit it. I followed Françoise, looking over my shoulder one last time for Drake. We slipped inside the Louvre through the door Ben was holding open, into a narrow corridor.

Ben was instantly up in my face. "What are you two doing here? It's a good thing I saved you. Don't you know that Drake is right outside?"

"Which is why we're in here with you." My face was inches from his. I could see Ben's left eye was twitching. He looked tired. "So are you going to turn us over to Drake now?"

"That's a negative." Ben stepped back. "Infiltrating Drake's organization was my top secret mission. To get the Dangerous Double to a secure location."

"Really? Seems like teaming up with the bad guy is the worst way to do that."

"Actually, it's pretty smart," Françoise said next to me. "Drake is after the Dangerous Double, too. Joining him would let you snatch the painting out of his hands as soon as he got it."

"Thanks for the support, Françoise."

"She's right." Ben nodded. "After we visited the bakery, Pandora set up the exchange. But we all knew it was a doomed effort. Then Agent Fullerton told me Albert Black had decided the best way to get to the Dangerous Double was for me to go deep undercover. Top secret. No contact with the Pandora team."

"But Albert Black knew nothing about this," I said.

Ben actually looked embarrassed as he continued. "By the time I figured that out, you'd checked me out of the Princesse Hotel, and I was being interrogated by Albert Black," Ben said. "Agent Fullerton even had me believing that I couldn't trust Albert Black, that he was the one who was crooked."

"So you were double-crossed," Françoise said, sounding sympathetic.

"That's correct," Benjamin Green said.

"We're supposed to believe you were one of the good guys all along?" I couldn't help feeling irritated.

"It doesn't matter what you believe." Ben's face hardened. "What matters is finishing our mission: to find the evil *Mona Lisa* and keep everyone safe."

"Super-Agent Ben, to the rescue," I joked, but he ignored me. Françoise told him about the clue we found in the tunnels.

"Hmmm, do you know anyone with the initials *NW*?" Ben asked, crossing his arms with a serious frown on his face.

"Actually, Linc figured out that *NW* stands for *northwest*, like on a compass," Françoise said. "There's a gift shop northwest of the pyramid. We think my father hid the evil *Mona Lisa* there."

"Nice job, Baker." Ben slapped my shoulder.

"Don't sound so surprised."

"Let's not waste any more time standing around," Ben said.

"I couldn't agree more." The guy was getting on my nerves. "Let's get to the gift shop already, before Drake finds us."

Ben and I followed Françoise past a whole bunch of Roman statues, marble columns, high ceilings with gold-leaf detail—enough to make you dizzy. Luckily, the hall was deserted. We were so busy looking back for Drake, that when we turned left, we walked right into a group of guards.

One of them looked up and raised an eyebrow. He said something in French, and all the guards turned to face us. There was nowhere to hide.

Françoise smiled. "We lost our parents," she said.

I'm pretty sure Ben and I were both holding our breaths, waiting for these guards to come over and handcuff us or something. Neither one of us had the guts to say anything or make a run for it. Let's face it, we were busted.

But then one of the guards smiled. "How did you kids manage to miss the fire alarm evacuation?" He shook his head. "I'll take you outside."

"Actually, I think they're in the gift shop," I tried. I took my phone out my pocket. "Mom just called me and told me so."

The guard frowned, then motioned for us to follow him. "We make it quick, yes?"

THURSDAY, 12:30 P.M.

THERE'S SOMETHING REALLY COOL ABOUT
being in a museum as grand as the Louvre when it's closed, and only a few guards are around. Our footsteps echoed as we made our way down the stairs, to the massive lobby under the pyramid. It was almost like being in church or at the ocean—it made me feel small. I thought of Grandpa, and hoped he was okay.

And I hoped we could fib our way inside that gift shop.

"There it is," the guard said once we got to the north end of the hallway—northwest, I guessed, thinking of Dad's compass.

At the entrance there was an old lady, with silver hair that looked like it had been set with at least half a container of hairspray. She had a small pin in the shape of a flame on the lapel of her pink dress.

The guard spoke to her in French. The gift shop lady must've said the right thing, because he nodded and took off.

"I'm Madame Basque," the lady said as she shook Françoise's hand. "I'm a friend of your father's."

"She's the kind lady." I was feeling pretty smart right about then.

Madame Basque blinked, looking at Ben and me. "Twins. How fascinating."

"We're not twins, actually," I argued. "We just look alike."

"You copied me," Ben said.

"Only because I had to."

"Guys!" Françoise smacked me on the shoulder. "Seriously." To Madame Basque, "My father sent me here for something. A painting."

Madame Basque smiled at Françoise. "You're here for your package." Françoise nodded.

"Follow me." We followed her down a narrow hallway. "The storage room is back here." The room was the size of Dad's auto shop and was lit by just a dangling bulb, casting shadows across rows and rows of boxes, storage racks full of snow globes, and big replicas of the Eiffel Tower.

"Which box is it?" Françoise asked Madame Basque.

"He didn't tell me. But he marked the box with a red flame symbol—just in case I would run across it. Not that I've seen it." Madame Basque sighed. "For my safety, he said. I think your father was afraid whoever is after the painting would come here and make me tell."

"It'll take hours to go through all these boxes!" Françoise was losing it a little now. "We don't have time for that. How am I supposed to find it?"

"With Henry's help," I said, and pulled the Double Detector from my cargo pants' pocket. I punched the blue button four times. Waited for the blue screen to show, hoping Henry would come through for us.

Now, you knew he would, right? Henry is a genius. The screen showed a bright red rectangle, in the far right corner of the stockroom.

"Tell Henry he gets free croissants for life!" Françoise rushed over to the stack of boxes, and with Ben's help she manuevered the one that held the evil *Mona Lisa* free. Sure enough, there was a little red flame drawn on it.

"Should we verify the contents?" Ben asked. It was the first time I'd heard him ask something, not order it.

Françoise dug into her pocket and pulled out the glasses, the ones her father had given her on the plane. Then she handed them to me. "You go ahead."

Ben crossed his arms, giving me a little glare. He obviously wasn't used to being the bystander.

I took the glasses, feeling my heart race as I pried the top off the box. "You know you're only letting me do this because you're too much of a chicken." But neither one of us laughed. With the help of Françoise and Ben (who looked away), I lifted the wooden frame from the box.

I looked at the painting, blurred by the old glasses. "Hey,

this one has eyebrows!"

Françoise laughed. "All right, let's pack her up now that we know it's the evil *Mona Lisa*."

We did, and Ben and I helped her lift the box. I was distracted by finding the evil historic treasure, because should I now turn the painting over to Drake to save Grandpa, knowing it might be used as a weapon? Much as I loved Grandpa, I knew I couldn't.

As we moved to leave, I heard a door slam shut behind us. And I turned to look at the face I saw when this all began, the face of the man who was supposed to protect me on this mission. Agent Fullerton.

He pointed a gun at us and smiled. "I knew I could count on you for a diversion. And then for Ben to lead me right here? It's too good to be true."

Ben looked embarrassed. "You followed me."

"Thanks a lot, Agent Green," I mumbled. I looked for a speedy escape, but there was none.

Agent Fullerton waved his gun. "Drop the box. The evil *Mona Lisa* is mine now."

42

THURSDAY, 12:45 P.M.

WE LOWERED THE BOX. WHEN SOMEONE
is pointing a gun at you, you just don't get to argue or call the shots. And I knew Agent Fullerton well enough to know he wasn't afraid to use it.

"So that's why you wanted me to take Ben's place so bad?" I asked, looking for an escape. "To get me to find the evil *Mona Lisa*?"

Agent Fullerton laughed. "Heck, no. I didn't think you were smart enough. I just figured you would make for a good diversion, and I needed this operation to keep moving. That way Drake could get Mégère to give up the location of the Dangerous Double and the secret da Vinci collection, and then I'd take out Drake.

"Of course, that was plan A, which you ruined, Linc."

"You're welcome," I mumbled.

"But things turned out so much better! All I had to do was get Drake to send one of his guys to California to take your grandfather for a little ride."

"That was your idea?" I was about to jump Agent Fullerton, until I remembered the gun.

"Nothing like a little pressure on the family to get someone to do what you want. You led me right to the painting, and I get the five hundred million dollars." He checked his watch. "Just in time for the one o'clock transaction. Thanks, kids."

"You set me up?" Benjamin Green asked.

"You were just too good at your job," Agent Fullerton said with a shrug. "I needed you out of the way, and what better way than a 'deep undercover' mission." He laughed. "I knew you couldn't resist."

Ben swallowed. I actually felt bad for the guy now.

"So now what?" I asked Fullerton, looking for a way out of this jam. "You're going to sell this evil *Mona Lisa* to some bad guy who'll use it to hypnotize a mob? Don't you care about the death and destruction you'll cause?"

"What they do with it, I don't care." Agent Fullerton smiled. "I just want my money."

If only some of our secret agent buddies like Albert Black or Agent Stark were here to see the true Agent Fullerton. But they were probably busy being miffed at me for missing the cab that we were supposed to catch.

I saw Françoise's eyes dart, looking for a way out. But

there was nowhere to run, and there was no way we could take out Agent Fullerton. Unless . . .

"You know, I want to thank you," I said to Agent Fullerton as I watched him try to lift the box and hold the gun at the same time. Behind him, Madame Basque stood with her back against the storage racks, looking afraid and angry all at once. "That short training session with Henry was really great," I went on.

"Was it now? From what I remember, your study efforts weren't exactly stellar out there at the Ventura Hacienda." He gave me a smug smile.

"But I did learn something," I said, stepping closer, hoping Agent Fullerton wouldn't shoot me before I could move. And I tried to remember what Henry had said.

The key is to be smarter.

So I leaped forward and swooped Agent Fullerton's legs. Knocking him off balance, making him drop both the painting box and his gun. I did a Henry—and very successfully so for my first time, if I do say so myself.

Ben grabbed the gun, and Madame Basque jumped up behind Agent Fullerton, who was now on his knees. She lifted her right arm. And whacked him on the head with a big, heavy replica of the Eiffel Tower.

Françoise grabbed the box before it could fall. "Nice job, Madame Basque." She glanced at me. "You, too. And Ben." Agent Fullerton was on the floor, sprawled and bleeding slightly from the head.

Madame Basque straightened her dress and touched her

beehive hair. "Thank you, Françoise. Give me the gun, young man," she said to Ben. He reluctantly handed it to Madame Basque, and she took it like it was a dirty tissue. "You kids should go. I'll make sure the police take care of this man here."

We thanked Madame Basque again and exited the way we came in, after I got my backpack from coat check, then up the stairs and out through the glass pyramid. No Drake on the plaza this time. We made our way out of the Louvre courtyard, and to the street (Rue Whatever) along the Seine.

We found the evil *Mona Lisa*! The mission was a success, despite a crooked Agent Fullerton and pain-in-the-neck junior agent Benjamin Green.

And it wasn't any junior agent handbook or fake Benjamin Green that saved the day. I got the evil *Mona Lisa* back by solving clues with Françoise and doing crazy stuff, like throwing the Tickstick in a fountain and pulling a fire alarm. And taking down a crooked secret agent with the Henry.

Linc disasters had saved the world from bad guys. If only I could tell my friends back home.

Home. It was one o'clock. What would Drake do with Grandpa now that he didn't get his evil *Mona Lisa*?

"Hold up," I called after Françoise and Ben. I reached inside my pocket for my cell phone, and fumbled to dial my home number.

It rang five times. It might as well have been an eternity.

Finally, someone answered. "Hello, Linc?"

43

THURSDAY, 1:02 P.M.

"mom?"

"Hi, Linc." She sounded sleepy. "Why are you calling at four in the morning?"

"Sorry, Mom. You know boot camp. We get up early."

"How's boot camp?"

How's boot camp? Who cares—how's Grandpa? That's what I wanted to yell into the phone. But instead I asked, "Is Grandpa around?"

"What, you don't want to talk to your mother?" Mom sounded hurt. "Grandpa is asleep."

"You're sure?" My heart was pounding.

"Yes, of course I'm sure." Mom sighed.

I let out a deep sigh, too. Grandpa was okay! But how . . . ?

"He made my life miserable yesterday. We were so lucky to get a last-minute appointment for his hearing aid with this new company, D.E. Health Services—on the night before Thanksgiving no less!"

Lucky us. "So where did they take him?"

"Oh, nobody took him anywhere. Your grandfather," Mom went on, like our family relation made his behavior my fault somehow, "decided that the hospital taxi driver was a criminal. A hoodlum, he called this man."

"How did Grandpa know he was a bad guy?" I asked before I could think.

Thankfully, Mom didn't catch on. "Something about his car being too nice, and his shoes weren't right—you know how Grandpa watches those crime shows all day. He thinks he's a criminal profiler."

I laughed. "So what did he do?"

"When this poor driver tried to put him in the taxi, Grandpa hollered so loud, half the neighborhood came outside to see what the fuss was about." Mom groaned. "And he kicked the car—apparently, it was some sort of expensive German model. Then he elbowed the driver . . ."

Go, Grandpa!

"Mrs. Henderson next door called the police, thinking something fishy was going on. They called me at work. The driver left before the police got to the house, though—I hope he's not going to make us pay for the body damage on that car."

"But Grandpa is okay?"

"Of course, you know he's a tough guy. But I think he misses you."

After telling Mom I was on my way, I went to catch up with Françoise and Ben. They were trying to hold onto the evil *Mona Lisa* box and walk, but it was awkward, and we were tired.

"We need a taxi to get this home," she said. There were about a million other people along the street with the same idea, trying to flag down a cab.

But then I heard a car honk. And at the far end of the taxi lane, there was a giant hand with the flame tattooed on the wrist, waving out of a taxi's window.

"Guillaume," I said with a big grin on my face.

"Wait." Ben shoved me with his free arm. "We can't trust just any cabbie."

"He's a friend," I said, pushing Ben aside and grabbing the box. Françoise and I hurried to Guillaume's taxi and crawled in the back, holding the evil *Mona Lisa* box awkwardly across our laps. Ben joined us reluctantly.

"Good afternoon, my young friends!" Guillaume called, giving me a high five. "I heard about the alarm of fire, and I think: this is my friend Lincoln, causing problems at the Louvre."

"Thanks." And I meant it. Even if I was a trouble magnet, this time it was for a cause.

"And you have a twin." He shook Ben's hand.

"We're not twins, actually," Ben started, but Guillaume

had already turned around to put the cab in gear.

"I take you to the Maison du Mégère," Guillaume said as he yanked the steering wheel and pulled into traffic.

"Thanks for helping us," Françoise whispered.

Guillaume winked at her. "It is my honor. Sometimes, the dragon needs his protectors to spit fire."

"Wait, what's this business about the dragon and the protectors?" I felt like I was inside one of those big fat fantasy books all of a sudden.

Françoise smiled as she clutched her end of the box. "My great-great—well, my grandmother centuries ago had that nickname—the dragon. And it became the family name. But the name Mégère really means more like a nag or a pain-in-the-neck, to be honest," she added with a laugh. "Like Grandma."

No kidding.

"But who are the protectors?" Benjamin asked, stealing my question.

Guillaume had arrived at the bakery now. "We are simply friends of Françoise's father. Here to help him when needed."

"Like Pierre at the restaurant in Montmartre and that lady in the gift shop, Madame Basque," I said. "The flames—that's your trademark or whatever."

Guillaume nodded as he parked.

"One of the protectors called me, to tell me you were arriving, Lincoln. So I found you at the airport."

"The protectors? That was never in our intel reports," Ben said, crossing his arms. "We'll have to vet this information against our sources."

Françoise and I rolled our eyes at the same time.

"There are procedures, Baker. Protocol." Ben opened his door. "We'll take the box back to the Princesse."

"We're keeping it," Françoise said.

Ben shook his head. "You have a very dangerous weapon in that box. The U.S. government will have to destroy it."

Just when I thought Ben and Françoise might get into an actual fistfight over the Dangerous Double, another car pulled up behind us.

Trapping Guillaume's cab in front of the bakery.

"No!" Françoise clutched the box. "This is art—a historical artifact. Papa didn't trust me to find the painting, only for you to destroy it."

44

THURSDAY, 2 P.M.

THE PASSENGER DOOR OPENED, AND there was—Françoise's dad? Agent Stark followed, jumping out the back. Albert Black was right behind her (just a lot slower), and Henry, too.

"Papa?" Françoise hesitated only a second, but then left me with the evil *Mona Lisa*. While Françoise was hugging her dad, I got out with the box and caught up with Henry.

"I did it!" Henry poked me in the ribs, beaming with pride as he shook a spray bottle with some green liquid in it.

"You're not going to spray me with that, are you?"

"Her," Henry said. "I'm spraying her."

For a moment, I thought he was talking about Françoise,

but then I realized he pointed at the box with the evil *Mona Lisa* inside.

"I call it the Gaze Glaze." Then Henry went on about it being a special film to negate the refracting of light caused by the sfumato glazing, blah, blah science talk. I'd like to tell you exactly how it works, but it's Henry magic—that's all I can say. The short version: the Mégère family would get their *Mona Lisa* back, minus the evil power.

"How did you guys find Françoise's dad?" I asked.

"Because of you!" Henry slapped me on the shoulder as we watched Françoise talking with her dad. "I built another tracking device. So we found the Drake guys' rental car—remember how you stuck the sticker in the trunk of that car?"

How could I forget?

"And Mégère—turns out he was staying at a friend's house just outside the city," Henry said. "We went to get him as soon as I finished work on the Gaze Glaze."

"Nice job, Henry. And you, too, Baker," Ben said, nodding, looking serious as always. As much as I wanted to roll my eyes, I figured I should shut up and take the compliment this time.

So with all this good news, we did what all super top-secret, Dangerous Double–hunting government operations do.

We had a bakery party. After Henry sprayed the evil *Mona Lisa* with his Gaze Glaze, we celebrated the mission's success. There was French bread, cheeses, this stuff called pâté that had to be the best thing I ever tasted, chocolates, croissants—I know, your mouth is watering, right? Us kids had orange juice to drink and the adults had wine. Françoise's grandma was making sure there was plenty to eat while yelling at Albert Black in French for trying to light a cigar in the kitchen.

"I guess this means no more secret agent life for you." Françoise refilled my orange juice.

"I'm okay," I said—and I was. I mean, on paper it might seem cool to jump from a plane and run from bad guys, but in reality it's dangerous. And tiring. "I'm not exactly Benjamin Green over there."

We both looked across the room, where Ben was flipping through some sort of file.

"Well, I'm glad you're not him," Françoise said. "If it weren't for you . . . Well, thanks."

"For putting the sticker inside your dad's jacket?" I shrugged.

She was about to say something, but then her father joined us and shook my hand. "Thank you, Lincoln. For taking care of Françoise."

Françoise rolled her eyes and walked away to help her grandmother.

"She doesn't need any help, Mr. Mégère," I said. Maybe Françoise's dad had not seen her wield a stick. "So how did you manage to get away from Drake—I mean your brother, Jules."

Mégère smiled. "They were so busy fighting, I simply made a run for it when we landed. Then I called one of my friends, to hide out. But thanks to your friend Henry, I didn't have to hide out for long. The Pandora agents came to find me, and told me that Henry had found a way to make the dangerous painting safe."

"That Gaze Glaze is pretty genius."

Mégère talked about bringing back the artifacts into the Vault, or maybe loaning them out to the Louvre so people could enjoy them. Except for the evil *Mona Lisa*—the Dangerous Double had to stay a secret. We all toasted with juice and wine, and after cleaning out the Mégère pastry supply, Pandora took off to catch a plane.

So that's how it all went down. How I went from Chicken Boy, expelled middle school eighth grader and all-around troublemaker, to junior agent. Even if it was for less than a week. I told you it was life changing.

But then that night, I went home to be just Linc Baker again. I mean, you didn't really think the government would keep me on as a junior agent when they had Benjamin Green, right?

Exactly.

EPILOGUE

PLACE: SAM'S HOUSE

TIME: A FEW WEEKS LATER

STATUS: KICKING SAM'S AND DARYL'S BUTTS AT RACING MANIA EIGHT

"DUDE, NO WAY!" DARYL PRETENDED TO throw his remote across the room.

"Thank you, thank you." I bowed like I was an actor onstage. Hey—there's nothing wrong with taking the credit when it's due.

"For someone who doesn't have his own Xbox, you sure know how to play." Sam turned the system off.

"I do my best." I handed him my remote and checked my watch. "I better get going. Mom's actually home for dinner." Ever since I got back home from "boot camp," she'd picked up extra classes to finish her degree to be a nurse-practitioner, so family dinners were rare. I think she thought I was doing better.

And I was. No more Farmer Johnson lawsuit—Pandora had made good on their promise to make it go away. I was careful not to get in trouble again. I mean, no one actually knew that it was me who switched out the sixth-grade English test for a first-grade one. And that little incident with the runaway sheep during the December play—well, I'll save you the details on that one. Let's just say there was no evidence of my guilt.

I was doing great. My grades were just about good enough to pass sixth grade, and my homework was sort of on time—I was a new Linc Baker. As far as my adventures as a Benjamin Green double, that all seemed like long ago already. I'd almost forgotten how good those croissants tasted, and how cramped the trunk of a compact rental car was.

"See you tomorrow, Linc." Sam showed me out in a hurry—I was pretty sure he would get right back to Racing Mania so he could at least beat Daryl. I was about to turn around and knock on Sam's door to call him out on his chicken attitude when I caught a glimpse of something unusual but familiar.

Down the street, a black car was parked near the curb. Headlights on, even though it wasn't dark outside yet. Tinted glass.

I hesitated, then dropped my skateboard, and rolled closer. It couldn't be—could it?

But it was. Agent Stark opened the driver's-side door and waited for me to approach. She didn't say anything until I got into the car, but then you know why she was there, right?

Pandora had a new case—and let me tell you, it made the Paris mission seem like a kindergarten field trip.

MORSE CODE KEY:

A . _
B _ . . .
C _ . _ .
D _ . .
E .
F . . _ .
G _ _ .
H . . . .
I . .
J . _ _ _
K _ . _
L . _ . .
M _ _

N _ .
O _ _ _
P . _ _ .
Q _ _ . _
R . _ .
S . . .
T _
U . . _
V . . . _
W . _ _
X _ . . _
Y _ . _ _
Z _ _ . .

PIGPEN CIPHER:

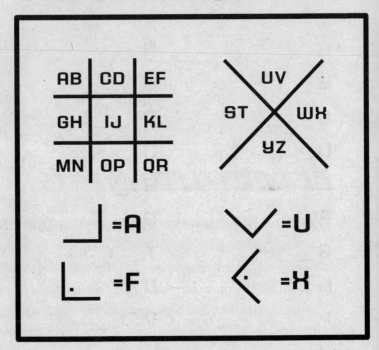

FOR MORE INFORMATION ABOUT HOBO SIGNS VISIT:

WWW.DOUBLEVISIONBOOKS.COM

ACKNOWLEDGMENTS

THE COVER MAY SAY THAT THIS BOOK IS written by F. T. Bradley, but the *T* really stands for the team of people who helped me get it done. This book would simply not be without them, so here are my humble thanks.

First, I want to thank my agent, Stephen Barbara, for believing I could do this even when I sometimes had my doubts. You rock, Stephen. Many thanks to everyone at Foundry for having my back.

Every writer needs an editor, and mine is simply the best. Ever. Barbara Lalicki, I smile every time you call, because I'm always excited to get back to work after we talk. I still pinch myself for having you as an editor, as well as Andrew Harwell and Jon Howard and everyone at Harper Children's. I'm so very fortunate.

I owe my writer friends big thanks for their support: Deb, Jenny, Shane, Mary, Ali, Bret, Laurel, John, Robin—I could add enough names to fill another book. Thanks for listening to me whine and for raising a glass when things looked up. Thanks to Pikes Peak Writers for the cheers.

Thanks to short story publications like *Stories for Children Magazine, The Thrilling Detective,* and *Versal* for giving me my first credits. Without your encouragement, I would have quit long ago.

Hugs to my family in Holland for always being proud of me. Xena (the cat): thanks for sitting on my lap at 4 a.m. to make sure I got the work done. And lastly, thank you to Jason, Tyne, and Nika, for understanding when I needed to hang out with Linc. I hope you found the story worth it.

**TURN THE PAGE FOR A SNEAK PEEK
AT THE NEXT ACTION-PACKED
SPY ADVENTURE**

DOUBLE VISION:
CODE NAME 711!

1

SUNDAY, 5:41 P.M.

YOU KNOW THE DAYS WHEN EVERYTHING
is going perfectly? I was having one of those that Sunday. I'd
just creamed Sam and Daryl at Racing Mania Eight, I was on
track with school stuff (or close enough anyway), and Mom
was cooking dinner since she had no classes and only one
shift at the hospital that day. I would be home before six to set
the table, so extra dessert for me. Life was good.

I rode my skateboard away from Sam's house, going extra
fast down the hill. But when I saw the black sedan at the end
of his block, I slowed. Wondered if maybe my gut was wrong.

Maybe this was some guy who was really into tinted windows. Maybe I should cross the street (safety and all that) and
speed up. There was a plate of spaghetti and meatballs waiting

for me. Chocolate cream pie for dessert. Just because there was a black car parked on my expected route home didn't mean that Pandora had come for me.

But then the driver's side door opened. A black lace-up shoe stepped on the pavement—a woman's shoe, but not the girlie type. Sensible footwear, made to catch a bad guy. Secret agent shoes.

Agent Stark got out of the car and gave me a little nod. And I knew my gut was spot-on: *Pandora was back*.

I got off my board and carried it as I walked toward her. "Hey, Agent Stark. You must be here for my mom's spaghetti dinner."

"Afraid not." She scanned the street, but the place was quiet. "Why don't you get in, and I'll drive you home."

Now, ordinarily it's a really bad idea to get into someone's car, even if you know who they are. Any kid knows that. And my board was just fine for getting me where I needed to be.

But this was Pandora's Agent Stark. If she came all the way to Lompoc, California, to talk to me, something had to be up. I had that familiar sense of dread and excitement in the pit of my stomach as I got into the dark sedan.

I put on my seat belt and tucked my board in the back of the car. "If you think I'm coming with you to pretend to be Benjamin Green again, you can forget it." Ben Green is this junior secret agent who looks just like me. On my first mission for Pandora, I took his place when he went missing.

"I wish I could forget it." Agent Stark sighed and put the car in drive. She doesn't really like hanging out with kids—in fact, she doesn't really like anything as far as I know. Agent

Stark is one of those humorless government agent types: brown hair always in a bun and never a smile. "But Albert Black sent me."

"Why didn't he come himself?" I asked, even though I knew he was Pandora's head honcho.

"He's meeting with the president." Agent Stark stopped at a yellow light.

"President of what?"

"The United States of America."

My jaw dropped. "President Griffin *herself*?"

"Why is that so surprising to you?" Agent Stark gave me an irritated glance. "Pandora is vital to national security. Black and President Griffin are going over mission strategy."

I almost asked her what the mission was but then stopped myself. The last time I joined Pandora, I was chased by bad guys in Paris and ended up jumping from an airplane. I know secret agent life sounds really exciting, but almost getting skewered by the Eiffel Tower is not. "I thought you had Benjamin Green for this."

Agent Stark hesitated. I could see she was thinking about what to say as the light turned green. "He's on another case. In fact, all of Pandora's other teams are on vital missions. We're it."

"So you need Agent Linc Baker, huh?"

"That's right. We need your special skills."

"And it's just me, no Ben."

"Yes." Agent Stark pulled over at the end of my street. "Can we count on you?"

"What's the case?"

Stark reached to the backseat and grabbed a blue folder. There were CLASSIFIED stamps all over it. "Here." She tossed it on my lap.

I opened it and got confused pretty quick. I learned from my previous run with Pandora that there's lots of boring paperwork and forms with mumbo jumbo no one outside the government gets.

"Flip to the printout of the email," Stark said.

I did and read the page:

TO: Mustang
FROM: Dagger
On schedule for Thurs @7 termination of POTUS and family.
Weapon will be retrieved in 48. The Washington is within reach.
Retain cover.

Huh?

"I have no idea what this means," I said. "What's POTUS?"

"That's what we call the president." Stark glanced to her rearview mirror, like someone out on Sam's street could be following us. "The email was intercepted and reported in the Presidential Daily Brief—it came straight from the director of National Intelligence."

"Something's planned for Thursday. *Termination*. Then it hit me. "Dagger wants to kill the president!"

Stark nodded. "And her family."

4

From watching TV, I knew President Griffin had a husband and a daughter, Amy, who was roughly my age. "Don't they have Secret Service and the FBI or whatever to protect them?"

"They do," Stark said. "But cutbacks have left them with reduced manpower. And this is serious enough that the president personally requested Pandora's help. There's a costume ball planned for Thursday at seven, in honor of Celebrating America's History Week. We think that's when Dagger plans to strike."

"Why did the president request Pandora?"

Stark shifted in her seat. "I don't know. Albert Black is keeping this case close to the chest." She sounded a little annoyed. "I'm sure we'll find out more once we get to Washington."

"So I'm supposed to just come along, without knowing what the case is."

"It's a few days in Washington, DC," Agent Stark said. "A vacation on us. You'll be back on a plane by Friday. And I'll even call your school so you won't get in trouble."

Something told me it wouldn't be that easy. But then I was reminded of this big history test I had on Wednesday. It was a killer, on the Revolutionary War and the Founding Fathers—and I'd studied for roughly five minutes so far.

This could be the break I needed. "I'll do it," I said. "I want just one thing." I told Agent Stark about the test.

"Consider it done. I'll get you an A."

"Make it a B-minus." I reached for my skateboard in the

back and opened my door. "Can't have Mom getting suspicious." *Mom and Dad.* "Wait—how am I going to explain this trip to Washington, DC, to my parents?"

"Say it's a science fair."

"I stink at science."

She cocked her head, like she was thinking. "Spelling bee?"

I shook my head. "Even worse."

"Is there *anything* you're good at?"

Racing Mania Eight. Skateboarding. Eating ten fries in one bite. Getting into trouble. "Not really."

Agent Stark shook her head. "I don't know, Linc. You're a smart kid."

"I am?"

"Creative, too. So make something up."

2

I SHOULD PROBABLY MENTION THAT making stuff up is something of a specialty of mine. Sure, I get into trouble sometimes, but I have good reasons. Someone had to prove to Mr. Finch that if you put more Mentos in a Coke bottle, the soda sprays higher. And I've talked my way from a D to a C-minus a few times already, so when Agent Stark told me to make something up, she knew I had the chops to pull it off.

Need a story? Leave it to Linc.

But for some reason, I couldn't think of one excuse that would convince Mom and Dad to let me take off to Washington, DC, for a week. As I chomped down on my third juicy meatball at dinner that night, the lies weren't coming to me.

7

It was kind of alarming, to tell you the truth. Like Spider-Man losing his superpowers.

"You're quiet tonight, Lincoln." Mom smiled at me from across the table. "Everything okay with your friends?"

"Sure. Yeah."

Grandpa muttered something cranky next to me. He thinks playing Racing Mania Eight on the Xbox is a waste of time—typical attitude of people who don't know the skill it takes to level up twice in an afternoon. Grandpa is more into old-school entertainment. Like five-thousand-piece puzzles and watching ancient movies with gangsters in them.

Mom squinted. "There's something going on. . . . Wait—did you get a bad grade?" Her smile dropped.

"No, no." I had to tell them something. Come up with some story before I lost my chance at chocolate cream pie. "Actually, there's one thing," I said, thinking maybe I could just wing it. "It's a trip."

"A field trip?" Dad lowered his fork. My last field trip didn't go so well, so he had reason to be worried.

"No, more like an overnight excursion," I said. Good spin, even if I do say so myself.

"During a school week?" Mom raised her eyebrow. I swear, she's like a human lie detector. "I thought you had a history test."

"This is for history, actually. It's a trip to the White House." Technically, that wasn't even a lie.

Dad lowered his fork. "You're not talking about the Junior Presidents Club, are you?"

Huh?

8

Mom grinned from ear to ear. "Is that it, Linc?"

Junior Presidents Club—what on earth was that? I stuffed a forkful of pasta in my mouth to cover my confusion.

"What's this Presidents Club?" Grandpa asked. Thank goodness for Grandpa, because I was flying blind here.

"There was a report on the news about it a few weeks ago. It's a short internship for promising young students," Dad explained to Grandpa, who looked like he thought it was just a load of nonsense. But then that was Grandpa's general expression, even when you told him the sky was blue. "President Griffin hosts a group of middle schoolers for a week so they can watch the government at work. The kids get to shadow staff members, tour the White House—it's a really great opportunity. On completion of the program, they get a certificate personally signed by the president."

Suddenly, I had six eyes on me as I swallowed my pasta.

Let's face it: I couldn't have come up with a better story myself. So I went right along and nodded—this Junior Presidents Club sounded like just the ticket.

Mom smiled wide. "Why didn't you say something sooner?"

"I guess I was waiting for dessert," I fibbed.

Mom gave me the last meatball. For dessert, I had two extra-large slices of chocolate cream pie. After a really long and boring story from Dad about how he once made it to the spelling bee quarter-finals, we cleared the table. And I was back to feeling life was perfect.

But things were about to go downhill—fast.